A Darker Shade of Midnight

LYNN EMERY

DEDICATION

This book is a homage to the storytellers in my family. They gave me a love of the fine art of passing on tales of drama, love, betrayal, friendship, and strange happenings so one could explain

Prologue

LaShaun lit a long tapered white candle on the altar and sat down on a bench near the front of The Immaculate Heart of Mary Church in Los Angeles. The white marble statue softly reflected dozens of flames. The Virgin Mary looked down with a serene expression of acceptance and forgiveness. No matter what sins those who sought refuge had committed, she was willing to absolve. LaShaun tried to pray, but the words stuck in her throat.

"Hello, child," a quiet voice spoke with the lilt of a Latino accent.

The rustle of fabric caused the flames to waver. LaShaun looked up. The nun wore an expression not unlike the statue before them. Even at fifty Sister Adalia had the smooth brown skin of a woman ten years younger.

"I'm okay, Sister." LaShaun started to stand, but a light touch on her shoulder from the nun's hand stopped her.

"You're here because your heart is at peace?"

"You know me too well," LaShaun replied with a

smile that soon faded. "I have to go home."

"I see." Sister Adalia sat next to her with a soft sigh. "You've come a long way, not just in miles. Maybe it's time."

"Monmon Odette needs me. No matter what our differences, she loves me. But if I go back... will I be tempted to slip into my old ways?" LaShaun fingered the red onyx beads of the bracelet on her right wrist. The golden cross that dangled from it felt comforting against her skin.

"You're a changed person. That change goes deeper than you think," Sister Adalia said.

"And the spirit I summoned?" LaShaun whispered the forbidden truth that she had shared with Sister Adalia. Only one other person knew, Monmon Odette.

"We humans do more than enough evil on our own. Don't give the devil and his minions so much credit."

"You and I know there are angels. There are demons at work in the world as well. My family has mixed the old religions from Africa with Catholicism for generations. More than a few of us have paid the price. I can't run from fate anymore." LaShaun bowed her head.

"You needed that time and distance to find yourself. The strength of your ancestors is in your blood." Sister Adalia looked at the cross that hung on the wall in an alcove behind the altar.

"I hope you're right, sister." LaShaun raised her head to look at Sister Adalia, and then followed her gaze to the cross.

"Now faith is the substance of things hoped for, the evidence of things not seen," Sister Adalia quoted the scripture in a reverent tone.

"The old religion warns there is a price to pay for dealing with spirits. So does the Bible."

"Our Blessed Mother will protect and guide you. Of that I'm sure. However, if you need a human ear, call me. Better yet, send a text or a tweet. I've got my new smart phone. " Sister Adalia patted the pocket of her dark blue jumper.

LaShaun laughed. "Twenty-first century nun to the rescue."

"Our order already has a Facebook page," Sister Adalia said, laughing with her. They stood together and walked to the altar filled with lit candles.

"Thank you for being my friend." LaShaun squeezed her hand.

"I'm glad we met. You'll be just fine," Sister Adalia replied.

Before LaShaun could respond a gust of warm air pushed down the center aisle of the pews. The candle flames danced crazily, but didn't go out. The lights of the church dimmed and long shadows on the walls gave the impression of a crowd in the sanctuary. Sister Adalia gasped and made the sign of the cross. The warmth changed to a chill in seconds. Then the light grew strong again.

"May God be with you." Sister Adalia let go of LaShaun's hand. Her dark eyes sparkled with alarm.

With a nod goodbye, LaShaun left the church and went out into the crisp night air. She drove to the townhouse where she lived in the bedroom community of Hawaiian Gardens, California outside Los Angeles. She opened the front door just in time to pick up the ringing phone. A family member told her what she already had sensed There were dark, sad days ahead.

Chapter 1

LaShaun sat calm amid the bustling activity at the small sheriff's station. Apparently, folks got into a lot of mischief Saturday nights on the bayou. Despite being so busy, the deputies and civilian employees found time to shoot sideways looks in her direction. Likely only a few actually needed to be near the area where she was seated. With the exception of Deputy Myrtle Arceneaux, the only black female deputy on the force. Her copper brown skin blended with the tints in her hair. No doubt she had the duty of making sure LaShaun did not attempt to leave the premises. Deputy Arceneaux sat at a nearby desk rustling paperwork. Deputy Chase Broussard had pulled her over then had her follow him to the station. He was somewhere trying to figure out a way to charge LaShaun with a crime serious enough to make her spend the night in jail.

LaShaun wore an impassive expression, a skill she had learned as a girl at her grandmother's knee. Lucky for them Monmon Odette was seventy-seven and ailing or she'd have show up to quietly scare the jeebies out of them. Her ability to exact revenge using voodoo was legendary in Vermillion Parish, Louisiana. Monmon Odette loved playing the part of a modern Marie Leveau. Despite her circumstances, LaShaun laughed softly at the memory of how her grandmother relished the notoriety, and used it to great advantage. LaShaun fingered the necklace she wore.

The young secretary seated at the front desk stared. She seemed fascinated by the snake pendant. Made of silver with carnelian stones for eyes, it hung from a red leather cord. LaShaun transferred her placid gaze from a spot on the drab light green wall to the skinny blonde-haired clerk. The woman jumped and blinked rapidly when their gazes met.

"Hello, Darlene," LaShaun said quietly.

"How do you know my name," Darlene said, her voice squeaky and eyes wide.

"Name tag." LaShaun pointed to the brass plate fixed to a wooden bar on her desk.

Darlene blinked rapidly some more, then let out a high-pitched giggle. "Well duh, Darlene. Nobody needs a crystal ball to know that."

Another woman marched up. She looked ten years older than Darlene. Her too perfect red hair convinced LaShaun that it came from a bottle. Freckles covered her pale face. She gave LaShaun a brief sideways look then frowned at Darlene. "What are you doing?"

"Just being polite," Darlene replied. "LaShaun, this is Terry Ramirez. She works over in robbery and-"

"Stop chit chatting and get back to work." Terry jerked a thumb toward a stack of folders.

"Right," Darlene said obediently, but frowned when Terry turned her back. She stood, gathered folders, and gave LaShaun a wink before she strolled off.

"LaShaun?"

Turning toward the voice, LaShaun found herself face to face with Savannah St. Julien Honoré, her childhood nemesis growing up in Beau Chene.

Savannah's honey brown skin blended well with the golden highlights in her hair. She stood next to a sullen young woman. Terry lingered nearby and thumbed through papers on Darlene's desk.

"Hello, Savannah." LaShaun looked at her. Her long hair pulled back into ponytail, Savannah wore navy blue slacks, a crisp light blue shirt and carried a leather case. "You're representing a client? I thought you retired from the law to run the family business."

Savannah nodded to the young woman. "Go on, Nyla. Come to my office nine o'clock sharp tomorrow morning."

"Okay." Nyla strode off with one last scornful look around to let law enforcement know she didn't think much of them.

"I practice part-time, mostly pro bono for kids in trouble. You need a lawyer- again?" Savannah's expression implied she wasn't shocked.

"Not me. This is just a misunderstanding," LaShaun said.

"Sure it is," Savannah replied in a dry tone. "Sorry to hear about your grandmother being so sick."

LaShaun gazed at Savannah. She really meant it. Of course she did. Savannah had always been the "good girl", the polar opposite of what the town folk thought of LaShaun. "Thanks. She's gotten weaker, but she's strong willed."

"Yeah, everybody knows. So how long will you be in town?"

"Don't worry. We'll have time to do lunch and catch up on old times." LaShaun smiled.

"Definitely. Wait by the phone for that call." Savannah gave her a tight smile and walked off.

"See you later."

LaShaun waved to Savannah when she looked back once more before exiting the station. Terry stared at LaShaun across the room with a stony expression. Moments later Deputy Broussard strode toward her. She suspected he meant to shake her up with that harsh façade. Obviously Deputy Broussard had not done his research on her very well.

The tall husky deputy stood about three feet away. One hand was on the dark brown gun belt around his waist. He gave a curt gesture like a traffic cop directing cars. LaShaun did not miss the way Terry stood straighter and brushed two fingers through her hair when he got close to them. "Ms. Rousselle, this way please."

LaShaun walked close enough to brush her arm against his. "I most certainly will, Deputy Broussard. I'm going to cooperate fully."

Terry sucked in air like an angry vacuum cleaner. "Call if you need me to pull any reports or records."

"Thanks. I have everything I need already," Deputy Broussard said. He gestured for LaShaun to walk ahead of him.

"Nice meeting you." LaShaun smiled at Terry. She put a little extra sway to her jean- covered hips as she walked ahead of the deputy. A look back at the woman confirmed her suspicion. Terry would have gladly scratched out LaShaun's eyes.

"Third desk on the left, ma'am." Broussard gave a sharp nod.

"All right, Deputy Broussard. My, my. All this attention because my rental SUV has a broken taillight. Must have happened on the road here. Nice to know

Vermillion Parish is protected against jagged plastic."
LaShaun knew getting smart might cause her more
trouble. Still she liked seeing Broussard's jaw muscle
cramp up when she refused to cower. She had inherited
a smart mouth from her late mother, Francine.
Something Monmon Odette chastised her for on
numerous occasions.

"That bag of weed has more to do with why you're
here, ma'am," a second deputy clipped back. He fell in
behind them as though assigned to LaShaun's case.

"Herbs," LaShaun corrected mildly. She followed
Broussard to another room. A scattering of three or four
deputies sat at desks completing reports or talking on
phones.

"We'll see," the other deputy replied.

Deputy Broussard didn't respond to his colleague's
comments. "Have a seat, ma'am."

LaShaun sat down and looked at the other deputy's
nametag. "I'm being arrested because I'm an old school
herbalist, Deputy Gautreau?"

"Them don't look like no Creole seasonings to me.
Now you just came from the airport from Los Angeles.
Lot of drugs pass through here from Texas, New
Mexico and California." Deputy Gautreau stood against
the wall and crossed his arms. "I'm not saying you're
some heavy duty drug dealer. Look, you like a little
recreational use, get amped up on the weekends with
some Acapulco gold maybe. I mean you only have a
few ounces. First offense gets you a five hundred dollar
fine and maybe six months in jail, unless we find
you've been picked up on previous drug charges."

"You won't. I don't even smoke tobacco. I allow
nothing and no one to take control of me, Deputy

Broussard," LaShaun said quietly.

"But you have been arrested before in this parish," Gautreau said.

"I was questioned," LaShaun said correcting him without a trace of anger in her tone.

"You were booked," Deputy Gautreau insisted, the inflection in his voice meant to needle her into reacting.

LaShaun ignored the attempt. "Since you're familiar with the case you know that the charges were dropped."

"Suspicion of murder. Pretty serious."

LaShaun caught Terry watching them from across the room and leaned toward Deputy Broussard. The V-neck of her red t-shirt didn't give him much of a view, but Terry couldn't see that from where she stood. "Lack of evidence," she murmured then pursed her lips.

"Which isn't the same as saying you were innocent of the charge," Deputy Gautreau shot back.

"Yes it is," LaShaun said softly. "As a law officer you must be familiar with the phrase innocent until *proven* guilty."

"Sometimes it just takes a little longer to build the case." Deputy Gautreau smiled at her.

. "I've got this one, okay?" Deputy Broussard turned in his chair sharply. He eyed the other man until Gautreau grunted, pushed off from the wall, and strolled off.

LaShaun forgot her game of driving the love struck secretary crazy. Interesting, she mused. The two men despised each other. She studied Deputy Brossard as though he were part of a police line-up, taking note of the tiny scar beneath his left eye. He had Cajun black eyes and curly black hair, his skin a light tan that was most likely from being in the sun. Back in the day she might have flirted with him. Broussard was handsome in a ramrod straight-arrow way. She didn't remember his face though. Of course eleven years had passed. Still the events that led up to her arrest played out in her dreams for years after, like a video in high definition.

"I didn't kill Claude Trosclair no matter what you've heard," LaShaun said.

She lowered her eyes then looked at him again. Broussard stared at her in silence for a few seconds, his gaze lingering on her lips. Like a tiny electric shock. LaShaun realized she wanted him to believe her. She'd always instantly disliked any symbol of authority. But they weren't usually this sexy. Footsteps and paper rustling broke the spell they seemed to be casting on each other.

"Here is the report from last shift on that burglary." Terry slapped a brown folder onto the desk between LaShaun and the deputy.

"Thanks, but I'm kinda busy right now, Terry. Give it to Myrtle if you don't mind." Deputy Broussard frowned then handed it back to the woman.

"Fine." Terry stomped off.

Deputy Broussard looked at LaShaun again. He tapped the keyboard of the computer on the desk. "You were saying."

"That I'm innocent." LaShaun said.

"Okay," he replied, his tone lawman neutral. "So tell me why you're back in Vermilion Parish."

LYNN EMERY

Chapter 2

"I— " LaShaun broke off when Deputy Broussard's boss strode in.

Sheriff Roman "Romey" Triche's hair was silvery white. When she'd left nine years ago, he still had traces of brunette mixed with the gray. At five feet eleven inches, he looked short next to Broussard. Still he had an air of authority that made him seem taller. He came straight toward them without looking left or right. The room got quiet. Even the phones stopped ringing. Darlene had abandoned her reception duties to watch the scene. Terry stayed to watch also, the scowl on her face directed at LaShaun. Deputy Arceneaux, followed Sheriff Triche. Deputy Gautreau joined them again as well.

"Evenin', LaShaun." Sheriff Triche nodded to her. "Sorry to hear 'bout your grandmother bein' so sick and all."

"Thank you, Sheriff," LaShaun nodded back to him. "You think I might get to see her tonight? I've had a long plane ride from L.A., and a long drive from New Orleans."

Sheriff Triche blew out a gust of air and looked at Deputy Broussard. His gray eyebrows pulled together in a frown. "Well?"

"Broken taillight, but more important a suspicious substance." Broussard pushed the clear plastic bag on top of the desk toward Sheriff Triche.

"I stopped at a shop in the French Quarter after I got in from New Orleans. Monmon loves the way I fix my special tea." LaShaun looked at Deputy Broussard.

"I use a mixture of chamomile, mint and ginger root. I could give you the recipe if you like."

"That's one of three I found." Broussard ignored her   dig.

"Humph." Sheriff Triche picked up the bag and opened it, took a sniff then closed it again

"I say send these over to the State Police lab for analysis." Gautreau struck a self-important pose. "Then we'll know what's what."

"Myrtle ain't got time to run no errands," Sheriff Triche said. "She's working on them burglaries. Something I thought you was helping her with."

"I will." Deputy Gautreau started to say more, but the Sheriff waved a hand at him.

"We can't be usin' up our measly budget on expensive State Police lab tests on tea leaves." Sheriff Triche took out a pinch of dried leaves from one of the bags and put it on his tongue.

"But boss— "

"This here ain't nothin' but a bunch of wild herbs from out in the swamp. My granny was a traiteur. Used to see her lay all kinds of plants out to dry. This here, use it for a tea to settle the stomach." Sheriff Triche repeated the taste test from the other two bags. "Herbs"

Gautreau drew himself up and his jaw muscle tightened again. "Well maybe so, but we better be sure with all the drugs coming through. We got a real problem in this parish. I'm gonna keep these."

Sheriff Triche puffed out a long-suffering sigh. "Right, law and order to impress the voters. Them same voters find out you wastin' their tax dollars on tea leaves and you'll hear from 'em. Once you find out these are just medicinal plants she'll get her property back."

"You're in charge," Gautreau replied in a dry tone.

"Yeah," Sheriff Triche said. He looked at Gautreau until the man walked off.

Deputy Broussard looked at LaShaun with curiosity. She could see the wheels turning as he wondered about her, and her past. She knew he was sorting through what he'd heard about the Rousselle family, and comparing that to his boss's behavior toward her.

"LaShaun, come talk with me a minute in my office." Sheriff Triche gestured for her to follow. His gaze sent a silent message at Deputy Arceneaux and she followed them.

"Glad to visit with you, Sheriff."

LaShaun walked between the sheriff and the female deputy. The audience sat still and quiet as though they were watching a drama unfold. When a phone rang a tall dark brown deputy swore and snatched up the receiver.

"Now I feel like I'm really in trouble. Or maybe I'm being treated special. Be careful, Sheriff Triche. Folks will talk when they hear about this, and I don't want Mrs. Triche mad at me," LaShaun joked.

Sheriff Triche only grunted in response. When they arrived at his office, he stood aside after opening the door. Half of one wall was glass with vinyl blinds hung to provide privacy if needed. Deputy Arceneaux nodded for LaShaun to go first.

"Thank you, ma'am. You're safe with me, Sheriff. You don't need Deputy Arceneaux here to protect your reputation."

"Getting more like your grandmother I see," Sheriff Triche retorted. He waited until Deputy Arceneaux closed the door before he went on.

"Was that meant as a compliment or insult?" LaShaun grinned at him.

"Both." Sheriff Triche squinted at her for a few seconds then his expression relaxed. "Damn it girl, you barely crossed the parish line and already you causin' me headaches."

"I'm so sorry. Never mind I've been sitting around this grim place for almost two hours being gawked at like a zoo animal." LaShaun crossed her arms. "Wonder who told that cute deputy to stop me?"

"Chase is doin' his job." Sheriff Triche gave a slight shrug when LaShaun arched an eyebrow. "You know how you left things. Not much has changed."

"Like I believe in coincidences. The Trosclair family still running things I see." LaShaun pressed her lips tight and gazed back at the sheriff.

Sheriff Triche looked at Deputy Arceneaux and seconds later she left quietly. The door made a soft bump as closed. The sheriff wiped a hand over his face and sighed.

"Don't start with the conspiracy theories, okay? I'm betting when Deputy Broussard brought you in somebody told him about you."

"Like Deputy Arceneaux? And I know she didn't go very far, so I'll keep my hands visible so she doesn't rush in here and jump me," LaShaun said. She didn't smile this time.

"You know damn well Myrtle don't gossip. One of the best officers I got. Chase ain't bad, just a little... intense." Sheriff Triche stood and went to a compact

20

refrigerator on a table in one corner of the wide office. He took out two bottles and closed it again. Then he grabbed an old-fashioned bottle opener and popped off the tops. "Have some Barq's Crème Soda. Still your favorite I bet. Got some corn chips in here, too."

LaShaun studied him as he came back and held one of the bottles to her. After a few seconds, she took it. "If you pull out onion dip and some lace napkins I'm gonna faint."

Sheriff Triche barked a gruff laugh. "We won't need the smelling salts then."

"So, you plan tell me who's still got me on their list?" LaShaun took a swig of crème soda and waited.

"We don't have that much time." Sheriff Triche put a toothpick in his mouth and chewed it for a few seconds. "But you got it right when you mentioned the Trosclair kin. Claude's brother and other relatives won't come at you in the open. Because of Quentin."

"My bad taste in men comes back to haunt me." LaShaun turned the cold, long-necked bottle of crème soda in her hands. "Be nice if you told me Quentin has moved out of town, and the Trosclair family isn't rich or powerful anymore."

"Would be nice, but it would be a lie." Sheriff Triche took out the toothpick and tossed it in the trash. "He's a Trosclair to the bone, thinks he owns the world and nobody can touch him."

Quentin Trosclair. LaShaun's former undercover lover and fellow suspect in the murder of his own grandfather. The alleged motive was money of course, and lots of it. "The Trosclairs may not own the world, but they sure got a big piece of Vermillion Parish. Last time I checked Quentin hasn't spent even one minute in jail."

"Humph." Sheriff Triche's bushy gray eyebrows crunched until they looked like a wooly caterpillar. He rubbed his hands together. Frustration that he hadn't been able to clamp handcuffs on Quentin radiated from him in a red-hot aura.

"As fun as this stroll down memory lane is, Sheriff, I'd rather be on my way." LaShaun set the soda bottle down on his desk. "If y'all don't have evidence to arrest me on something I'm leaving."

"Everybody around town figured you'd be back because your grandmamma is real sick. But Deputy Broussard really did stop you for that broken taillight. We've picked up more than a few drug runners and fugitives from traffic stops."

"If you say so." LaShaun knew he made sense, but wasn't ready to concede just yet. "But he did recognize my name."

"Rousselle name carries its own unique reputation you might say. So yeah, when he called it in I'm sure somebody gave him the 411." Sheriff Triche nodded. "Hell, I knew you were back about two minutes after Chase called in your driver's license number."

"I didn't miss living in a fish bowl," LaShaun retorted.

"The Trosclair family has powerful friends. Not that you didn't piss off a few more folks in your time," Sheriff Triche said. "With your grandmamma being down sick folks might feel little safe comin' at ya. If you know what I mean."

LaShaun stood. "I'm here to spend time with Monmon Odette, that's all. If you don't mind I'd like to go now."

Sheriff Triche stood. "One more thing, your family ain't been exactly harmonious. I heard talk about feuds over her land and such."

"There's no place like home," LaShaun said with a grunt. "Thanks for the warning. By the way, why are you giving me the heads up on all this stuff?"

"Hoping it might help ward off another big mess. I've dropped a few words of warnin' to various other citizens, too." Sheriff Triche tapped a forefinger against his temple.

"You've got a sharp brain inside that old Cajun head." LaShaun put her hands on her hips.

"Steer clear of Quentin and trouble."

"Yes, sir." LaShaun snapped to attention and gave him a military salute.

Sheriff Triche shook his head and pointed to the door. "Lawd, have mercy. I'm about to retire in a few months, and you come back to town. Go on then."

LaShaun lowered her hand and gazed back at him. "Sheriff, if there's any trouble it won't be because I started it."

"Humph." The sheriff didn't sound convinced as he followed her out of his office.

Deputy Arceneaux had been leaning against the wall of the hallway. She stood straight when she saw them and fell in step behind Sheriff Triche.

"I feel so safe with all this police presence," LaShaun joked.

The three of them reached the big open room. Once again, all chatter and noise quieted as they entered. Deputy Broussard was talking to Deputy Gautreau, and the exchange didn't look friendly. LaShaun once again picked up on the bad blood between them.

"Sir," Deputy Broussard said, and looked at his boss expectantly.

"Until you find out these ain't illegal substances LaShaun can go on to Monmon Odette's."

"Okay." Deputy Broussard nodded.

"But she could leave anytime," Gautreau said.

"Right now we don't have enough to hold her. I still know the law even with one foot out the door." Sheriff Triche rubbed his forehead and winced. "Now just do what I say."

"My grandmother is seriously ill, so I have no plans to leave for at least two weeks." LaShaun gazed at Sheriff Triche and then at Deputy Gautreau.

"No probable cause." Sheriff Triche gestured for LaShaun to follow him.

"I didn't write out the ticket for that broken taillight." Deputy Broussard wrote the ticket. He tore off the short white piece of paper and held it out to LaShaun. "You have to pay the fine or report to traffic court."

"I'll pay the fine since I'm guilty. But for the record if any other broken tail lights show up I didn't do it." LaShaun took the ticket and smiled at Deputy Broussard, her lips parted. He stared back at her mouth. "And you can't prove I did even if you try."

"Lawd, have mercy." Sheriff Triche muttered and heaved a sigh.

LaShaun flipped her fingertips at them as her only goodbye. Despite her insolent, hip-swaying exit from the Sheriff's station her legs felt shaky. When she reached the parking lot LaShaun took in a deep breath of the cool March night air. Once inside the Mercury Mariner, she exhaled and locked the door. Though she should have known better than to issue that challenge, LaShaun had been unable to stop herself. After all, she was Francine's daughter and Odette LaGrange Rousselle's granddaughter. Challenging authority was most likely coded into her DNA.

* * *

The digital clock glowing in soft green on her dashboard said it was almost eleven thirty. The dark night of rural Louisiana hugged the Mercury Mariner on all sides as she drove down the country highway. After another fifteen minutes of driving LaShaun turned off Highway 77 onto the black top road called Rousselle Lane. A few twists and turns brought her to Monmon Odette's driveway. A curtain twitched and moments later the front door cracked open. LaShaun opened the driver's side door and got out. Her cousin Rita stood in the doorway, the bright porch light washed over her. She put both hands on her wide hips.

"Monmon kept asking about you. She was about to make me call out the sheriff's department to find you." Rita crossed the screened porch and let the screen door slap shut behind her.

"Just so happens they could have told you exactly where I was. One of your diligent deputies hauled me in. Got three bags. Grab this little one. I'll get the others"

"Damn, that didn't take long. You already pissed somebody off?" Rita stared at her for a few seconds.

"I'm not that good at being bad." LaShaun handed Rita a bag. "How's Monmon been today?" LaShaun went to the rear of the SUV. She unlocked the hatch and picked up both suitcases.

"Sleeping a lot. She's getting weaker in body and mind. She talks a lot about the past, most of it in Creole French, so I can't understand. I fixed up your room." Rita didn't wait for her, but went up the porch steps and disappeared into the house.

"Thanks," LaShaun said to empty night air. She went inside and placed her bags in the hallway.

Not seeing her cousin, LaShaun followed the smell of food to the kitchen. She breathed in the scent of onions, peppers, and garlic. A large electric skilled was set to the warm setting. Inside was jambalaya. A woven basket held a loaf of French bread. Minutes later Rita came to the kitchen. Rita turned from the stove when LaShaun came in.

"Monmon fixed that for you. She wouldn't let me cook. Says she's the only one knows how to prepare your favorites." Rita's tone held an edge.

"She's got an iron will. How are you?" LaShaun tried to ease the tension that crackled in the air between them.

"I'm doing fine. Since you're here I'm moving back to my place." Rita turned to go.

"Hey, you don't have to leave tonight. There's plenty of room." LaShaun caught up with her halfway down the hall.

"I put clean towels in your bathroom."

LaShaun smiled at her. "C'mon, we can hang out and catch up."

"I'm going home. The home health aide is named Tasha Easley. She comes three times a week to help. And the nurse comes by to check her vitals once a week." Rita said.

"I really appreciate all you've done." LaShaun started to say more but Rita cut her off.

"Monmon Odette will want to spend time alone with you." Rita left was through the front door and in her Ford Mustang before LaShaun could say goodbye. The headlights flashed against the house as she turned the car around to leave.

LaShaun sighed as she locked the front door. She instinctively turned into the living room to her left. The sights and smells of her grandmother's house acted like a time machine. One long sofa sat against a wall. A painting of Monmon's house and part of the woods surrounding it hung just above it. Two other smaller paintings of bayou scenes hung on two other walls. Over the fireplace was a portrait of a breathtaking woman, Odette when she was a woman of thirty. A baby grand piano sat in one corner of the room. The polished walnut finish gleamed as always. Most people didn't know it, but Monmon Odette was an accomplished pianist. LaShaun went to it and traced the fingers of one hand along the carved music desk above the keys. Then she sat down and gently played the first few notes of "Over The Rainbow".

"Why you actin' like you scared of them keys? Play the song right. That's one of my favorites." Monmon Odette said from the doorway.

She leaned heavily to one side on a thick carved wooden cane. Her skin had the color and texture of ancient brown parchment. Her white hair was combed back, and her scalp showed through in spots where it had thinned. The dark eyes still hinted at some secret power. She wore stud earrings. The twin gold beads gleamed as she moved her head. Then she smiled with affection. The years seemed to slip away. A remnant of the beautiful woman she in the portrait came through. LaShaun once again knew why Monmon Odette was a legend in Vermilion Parish. Nothing short of magic seemed to flow from that smile. Yet, LaShaun also knew the truth.

Chapter 3

LaShaun answered by playing the song as though she were in a grand concert hall. She repeated the opening notes then let them tinkle like flowing water. Monmon Odette continued to smile as she sat down in the nearest stuffed chair. LaShaun ended the tune with a flourish that would have made any conductor proud.

"Humph, now you're just showin' off," Monmon Odette said when the final note died away. She put the walking cane aside and stretched out a hand to LaShaun. "Welcome home, my sweet baby girl."

LaShaun went to her. She kissed the hand that had guided her through childhood. Now the knuckles were knotted, the tapered fingers weakened by arthritis. Yet, the skin appeared strangely smooth.

"Bon soir, Monmon. You should be in bed." LaShaun kissed her forehead. She breathed in the familiar scent of Cashmere Bouquet. The fragrance of lavender and chamomile came from another era.

"So, you finally come home. To watch me die, eh?" Monmon Odette patted LaShaun's cheek.

"To celebrate your life, sweet mother," LaShaun whispered. A tear slipped down her face. No need to make pointless protestations otherwise. They both knew Monmon Odette's time on earth was growing shorter.

Monmon Odette shushed away her sadness with a soft hiss. She produced a scented lace handkerchief from the pocket of her robe and dabbed away the tear. LaShaun sat on the floor and rested her head in Monmon Odette's lap.

"Don't grieve just yet, Cher . The blood is still

runnin' warm in these old veins. I've got just enough time left I think."

"Time for what?" LaShaun toyed with the hem of her grandmother's cotton gingham robe.

"You'll know soon enough. But tonight you need rest after a long journey. You've come back home through time and space I think," Monmon Odette murmured.

LaShaun looked up at her. "Has anything changed here?"

Monmon Odette patted her shoulder as a signal she wanted to stand. With a short grunt from the effort, and a hand from LaShaun, she rose from the chair. Monmon Odette held LaShaun's arm as they walked down the hallway to her bedroom.

"Some things are eternal. The movement of the wind, the heat on the bayou when summer comes. All that is the same."

"The land stays the same if people don't ruin it. Like they ruin a lot of things," LaShaun said softly.

"Human nature doesn't change either, Cher ." Monmon stopped and gave LaShaun a sideways glance. "The same deadly sins rule a man's nature."

"And women," LaShaun added raising an eyebrow back at her.

Monmon Odette laughed and started walking again. "True. But age does make a difference. When you get to be old you look at things differently."

They arrived at the door to her grandmother's bedroom. As they entered, LaShaun let her go in first. Then she fluffed the down pillows as her grandmother sank onto the bed. LaShaun helped her remove the robe and ease back onto the pillows. Once she'd tucked the vintage quilt around Monmon Odette's chest her grandmother sighed.

"Thank you, sweet girl. Now sit with me awhile."

LaShaun sank onto the cushioned seat of a large oak rocking chair next to the bed. A Bible was on the nightstand. "Of course. Shall I read to you?"

"Non."

Monmon Odette closed her eyes after a few moments. LaShaun watched the slight rise and fall of her grandmother's chest. After a while, she gazed around. Monmon Odette had redecorated. Her grandmother had a fondness for antiques, history and tradition. Yet, Monmon Odette was no old lady clinging to the past. LaShaun smiled when she saw the combination radio and compact disc player on the other wide nightstand. The high tech device didn't clash with the country style décor. Curtains with a lovely old rose pattern on a cream background matched the quilt, the rug and pillow shams. An overhead cane ceiling fan looked old enough to have come from one of the plantation homes along Vermilion River. Then LaShaun saw the family photos on a round table. She left the rocker and went to it. Several pictures were sepia toned, taken before the turn of the last century. "Celie LeGrange, 1866-1932" was written at the bottom of one. Monmon Odette's mother. Jules Paul LeGrange, husband to Celie and Monmon Odette's father, stared stone-faced from another photo. An even older picture of a lovely woman dressed in a long dress and button top shoes sat next to it. LaShaun did not have to read the faint letters to know her. Acelie LeGrange stared at her descendant across time, two hundred years to be exact. LaShaun's mother stared from a photo taken in

1982. She looked beautiful in a flowered sundress. Francine stood next to a five year old LaShaun. Both wore forced smiles trying hard to look happy for the camera. LaShaun didn't remember that particular day, but she remembered her mother's overwrought disposition. Still in love with Antoine St. Julien even five years after he married another, Francine never found happiness.

"I'm glad you're home, Cher . Have you forgiven me?"

LaShaun looked up to find her grandmother's dark gaze fixed on her. "I didn't blame you for anything that happened to me, Monmon."

"Maybe you should have, and for your maman, too. So many mistakes and no time to fix them. But I may still have time to do some good for you." Monmon Odette inhaled deeply causing a rattling sound deep in her chest. She breathed out slowly then closed her eyes.

"I made my own choices, and my own mistakes." LaShaun blinked away tears.

Monmon Odette nodded without opening her eyes. "Maybe Le Bon Dieu will have mercy on this old woman."

"Just rest, sweet mother. I'll take care of you, and we'll laugh and sing Boozoo Chavis songs."

"Oh yeah," Monmon Odette murmured softly. She even hummed a bit of a zydeco tune as she drifted into sleep.

LaShaun crossed to the nightstand and turned off the lamp but left a nightlight on. The faint illumination cast shadows that heightened atmosphere of an eighteenth century Creole cottage. She watched her grandmother's chest rise and fall for a few seconds, and then tucked the quilt up closer to Monmon Odette's chin. LaShaun moved quietly across the rug-covered hardwood to the door.

"My lawyer will make things right Tuesday," Monmon Odette whispered.

"What?" LaShaun spun around.

Monmon Odette's head turned to the side on the pillow. She gave a contented sigh, and snuggled deeper into the covers. Seconds later she snored lightly. LaShaun could almost believe she'd imagined hearing her; except Monmon Odette wore a slight, sly smile as she slept. She resisted the urge to shake the old mischief-maker awake and get answers. Instead, she went to her bedroom. Fatigue forced her into pajamas and into bed. The sound of rushing wind lulled her to sleep. Her dreams were filled with misty swamp scenes, elusive voices, and the sense of being watched.

The next morning LaShaun pushed back the curtains in her bedroom. Maybe the bright Louisiana sunshine could banish the uneasy sense left behind by dreams she couldn't quite remember. After getting dressed, she went outside to the front porch. Her grandmother sat in the sunshine, a cup of hot coffee on the table next to her. Wrapped up in a crocheted shawl, Monmon Odette smiled when she saw her.

"Good morning, my bébé." Monmon Odette sighed, and then picked up her cup. She sipped and sighed again. "Nothing like good coffee on a pretty morning."

LaShaun looked around at the magnolia and oak trees scattered around the house. "I missed the green grass. Los Angeles is nice, but dry. You gotta have a lot of money to get your lawn green like this. Humph, you gotta have money to have a lawn." LaShaun walked to the edge of the porch and leaned on the railing.

"This is where you belong." Monmon Odette gazed off into the distance. Her voice held a strange quality, as though she spoke to someone else.

"Some might argue with that," LaShaun retorted with a smile. "I saw Savannah last night."

Monmon Odette waved a gnarled hand in dismissal. "Nonsense. This is your home."

"I caused a lot of trouble in my time. I had fun doing it sometimes." LaShaun winked at her grandmother.

"Girl, you still got the same spunk." Monmon Odette chuckled softly. Then her gaze shifted to the blacktop road. She pointed to an approaching car. "Now what would they want?"

The white Vermillion Parish Sheriff's department cruiser with green and blue lettering pulled up into the driveway. Deputy Broussard sat inside for a few seconds before he cut the engine. When he got out LaShaun noticed the long, lean frame wrapped in the dark khaki uniform. His wore an unreadable expression behind the dark sunglasses. He studied his surroundings then strode toward them.

"Morning ladies." Deputy Broussard nodded to Monmon Odette. "I was out this way, and decided to return your property. He held out a white plastic bag.

"Thanks." LaShaun looked inside at the three bags of herbs in cloth sacks. "I guess you found out I was telling the truth. Since you're not explaining my rights or taking out the handcuffs I mean." His crooked smile surprised and pleased LaShaun. Warmth from his curved lips seemed to snake out and curl around her body.

"Nothing but herbs, like you said. Sorry for the inconvenience." Deputy Broussard looked at Monmon Odette. "Hope you're feeling better, Mrs. Rousselle."

"Indeed I am, young man. Having my granddaughter home is a comfort." Monmon Odette smiled at him.

"I'm sure it is, ma'am." Deputy Broussard nodded respectfully.

Monmon Odette braced herself and stood up. "Let me look at my roses. I sure hope that cold weather didn't burn them." She started walking away toward the far end of the long porch.

"Monmon, what are you doing? Let me help you." LaShaun took a few steps when her grandmother scowled at her.

"I'm tired of everybody hovering over me like gnats. I can still enjoy a short stroll, and look at my own roses. Besides, don't be rude. This young man came way out here to bring back your belongings." Monmon Odette continued to walk as she spoke.

"She's very strong-willed," Deputy Broussard said.

"You have no idea. I could have picked up my herbs. Or were you curious about the infamous Rousselle family?" LaShaun dropped the bag on the small table next to the cane chairs.

His dark eyebrows went up over the sunglasses, and then he took them off. "Very curious to be honest, especially after the sheriff came to your defense."

"Oh really?" LaShaun leaned against a post and crossed her arms.

"According to him none of the evidence indicated

you killed Claude Trosclair. He also said the talk of you being a voodoo queen was a load of superstitious swamp country crap. That's a direct quote."

LaShaun laughed out loud. "Well, well. I never would have believed that Sheriff Triche would become my defender. Monmon, did you hear? The sheriff thinks the reports of my crimes and misdemeanors have been greatly exaggerated."

"Always said Roman Triche had sense," Monmon Odette called back.

"Anyway, I just wanted to say…" Deputy Broussard cleared his throat as LaShaun gazed at him. "Welcome back to Vermillion Parish."

"Thank you, Deputy Broussard. Maybe we'll run into each other again, hopefully under friendly circumstances." LaShaun's gaze followed the strong line of his jaw up to his dark eyes. He looked at her for several minutes before putting his sunglasses on again.

"Yes, ma'am." Deputy Broussard gave a sharp nod. "Good day, Mrs. Rousselle."

"Bye bye deputy. You come back anytime." Monmon Odette beamed at him.

She made her way back along the porch holding the wooden railing with one hand and her cane with the other. Moments later the cruiser disappeared around a curve in the driveway. Monmon Odette chuckled to herself as she gazed at LaShaun.

"What?" LaShaun placed one hand on her hip.

"That young man came way out here to bring you one little old bag. I feel safe knowing we got us such a considerate deputy. Yes indeed." Monmon Odette continued chuckling as she went inside.

"You're so funny, Monmon," LaShaun said. When

the screen door banged shut, LaShaun turned to look toward the road. And smiled.

* * *

LaShaun spent the next day settling in. True to her word, Rita moved back to her condo. She has arranged for a home health services for Monmon Odette. A nurse and nursing assistant would make regular visits. LaShaun became the contact person. Rita made the change with a matter-of-fact façade, but LaShaun detected the tension. In fact, all the smiling and cooperation as Rita handed over Monmon Odette's day-to-day care wore on LaShaun's nerves. Monmon Odette watched them both, saying nothing but knowing all. This family meeting with her lawyer was sure to be interesting.

At eight forty-five Tuesday morning. a sleek silver BMW sedan rolled up the driveway. Seconds later a tall, fine black man got out. LaShaun sat on the porch with the local newspaper. She dropped it on the table next to her chair, no longer interested in the new discount store opening or local high school sports. She watched Devin J. Martin, size up the house and surrounding land. His expression was unreadable behind the expensive sunglasses. Moments later he smiled as if aware he was being observed. He walked to the front porch, and LaShaun stood to greet him. His smile widened in appreciation when he saw her.

"Good morning, Mr. Martin. I'm LaShaun Rousselle, one of Mrs. Rousselle's granddaughters." LaShaun shook his hand. His skin was smooth and warm. He held her hand for the just the right amount of time. Not too long to be suggestive, yet long enough to leave the door open. She recognized a fellow player.

"Good morning." His handsome face registered surprise for an instant.

"Come in. I'll get you a cup of coffee. You've had a long drive from New Orleans."

"Thanks," he said as he followed her into the living room. He set his briefcase on the floor. Then he took off his sunglasses and carefully placed them in an inside pocket of his suit jacket. "Nice to meet you, Ms. Roussellc."

"And you." LaShaun turned to face him.

"So the stories are true. You're supernatural. You knew my name and that a cup of Louisiana dark roast would be appreciated."

She smiled at him. "Apparently not. I don't know what you like in your coffee."

Martin let out a throaty baritone laugh. "Nothing. I like it hot and strong."

"Then you're in luck. We can accommodate. Come on in." LaShaun stood aside against the open screen door as he entered.

With a confident stride, he went to the living room. The scent of his expensive cologne lingered. LaShaun let the screen door shut and watched him closely. Martin scanned the antiques in the foyer, pausing for a few seconds at a row of wood sculptures. LaShaun could almost hear his mind working, estimating what it could be worth in dollars.

"I see the lawyer made it." Rita stood on the porch wearing a slight smile. She opened the screen door and joined LaShaun in the hallway.

"You're both the first ones here." LaShaun said,

smiling back at her.

"Are we?" Rita glanced at her smart phone. "Guess I'm just used to getting up early. Is Monmon Odette in the living room yet?"

LaShaun raised an eyebrow at her attitude. "I'll get her. Go on in and have a seat. I'm fixing coffee now."

"Let me know if you need help," Rita said over her shoulder. Her offer seemed half-hearted because moments later she disappeared.

LaShaun went to the kitchen. She had a rolling wooden serving cart prepared with a carafe of hot coffee, cups, and beignets. Two elaborate ceramic bowls held sugar and real cream. Monmon Odette would not allow substitutes in her kitchen. As LaShaun came back down the hallway, she met Monmon Odette walking with care along the hardwood floor. The soft moccasins made her footsteps silent.

Monmon winked at LaShaun, put a finger to her lips, and whispered. "Listen, Cher , listen to them making plans. Shh." Indeed, they could hear the murmur of voices.

"What are you up to, Monmon?" LaShaun gazed at her through narrowed eyes. "You set up some mess inviting them here."

"Now why would I want to provoke my sweet relatives? Especially when they've been so good to me." Monmon Odette dark eyes sparkled with mirth. She gave a soft laugh then turned to leave.

Before LaShaun could say more Martin came through the archway. With a smooth, solicitous expression, he took Monmon Odette's arm and escorted her to the living room.

"Good morning, Mrs. Rousselle. How are you

feeling?"

"Hello, Mr. Martin. It was so good of you to come on short notice." Monmon Odette matched his smoothness with her own charm. "Such an important lawyer like you must be busy with more important matters in the big city."

"I was in the area on other business, so it was no trouble. Besides, your granddaughter has been very helpful." Martin helped Monmon Odette get settled in one of the high back upholstered chairs.

"LaShaun has spoken to you. How wonderful," Monmon Odette replied.

"No, I mean Ms. Rita here." Martin looked at Rita then back at Monmon Odette.

"I see. Tell me how she's been helpful." Monmon fixed a steady gaze on Rita.

"Ahem, I meant to say…" Martin looked at Rita again as if asking for help.

"Knock, knock. We're comin' in so don't shoot," a strong male voice boomed.

Moments later Theo Rousselle entered the room his head barely clearing the top of the doorframe. Albert, the quieter, more morose brother, followed behind, as usual. Monmon Odette's two surviving sons looked alike except for the difference in height.

"Hello, mama. LaShaun, look at you. I swear our niece gets prettier every year, don't she Albert?" Uncle Theo kissed LaShaun on the forehead like she was still the six year old he used to tickle.

"Welcome home." Uncle Albert blinked then gave her a brief hug.

"Thank you," LaShaun said. "My uncles are still as handsome as ever."

At six feet four, Uncle Theo still looked powerful even at sixty-one years old. Still his shoulders were more stooped than when she'd last seen him. With salt and pepper bushy hair cut short, he wore checked short-sleeved sport shirt and navy blue Dockers. He beamed at them all and at no one in particular. A shorter but just as formidable looking Albert was six years younger. He frowned around as though checking the room for threats as they entered the parlor.

"Mornin'," Uncle Albert grumbled. "How you feelin' this mornin', Mama?" Always dutiful, to a point, he kissed Monmon Odette on the check then stood back.

"Hey, good-lookin'," Uncle Theo said in his amiable manner. He kissed Monmon Odette on the cheek. "Somebody has been spreadin' lies, cause you lookin' way to young and spry to be sick."

"Hello, boys. Sit down. LaShaun gonna fix you some coffee." Monmon Odette waved her hand at LaShaun to reinforce her instructions.

As LaShaun passed around china cups of strong Louisiana dark roast coffee, more family arrived. Several cousins nodded to LaShaun, then crossed to Rita. They stood near a window talking low. After a few minutes Rita went back to sit on the sofa no far from Monmon Odette and the attorney. Aunt Leah came in with her oldest daughter Azalei. Aunt Leah's timid husband eased into the room as though determined to go unnoticed. Azalei walked over to LaShaun.

"Hello, cousin. Nice to see you again." Azalei didn't wait for a reply. She spun around and went to Monmon Odette. "Hello, dear grandmother. I'm so happy to see you doing better."

"Are you? Means you and your mama will have to wait a bit longer to inherit." Monmon Odette pursed her lips.

"We're more than willing to wait," Aunt Leah blurted out.

"How kind of you to be patient," Monmon Odette replied placidly. She looked up at her daughter. "I'll try not to test that patience much longer."

"I didn't mean we're sitting like vultures waiting for you to…" Aunt Leah blinked rapidly as Monmon Odette's lips curved up in a smile. "Of course you know that's not true."

"Hmm." Monmon Odette accepted a cup of coffee from Rita. "Thank you, dear. So Mr. Martin, shall we get started?" Conversation died away.

"Ah, right. I have the will you created. However your granddaughter has some changes." Martin cleared his throat.

LaShaun shrugged when everyone looked at her. "I don't know what he's talking about."

"When Monmon got so sick I took over. Her memory and judgment were affected by illness of course. So she gave me power of attorney for her business affairs and her medical needs," Rita said.

"Say what?" Aunt Leah blinked hard and fast as.

LaShaun gazed around at the faces. She could tell this was a news flash to all, and not a welcome one either. Monmon Odette seemed unfazed. LaShaun wondered if her grandmother even remembered signing those legal documents. Rita turned to Monmon Odette.

"You gave me power of attorney freely, isn't that right?" Rita spoke slowly as though she was being tolerant of her grandmother's mental shortcomings.

"Did I? I seem to recall something about that," Monmon Odette replied.

Rita looked at LaShaun first, then at the rest of her relatives. "Monmon Odette has good days, and bad days. In her best interest, I've taken control. Her assets have been placed in a trust, and I'm the sole trustee."

"What the hell?" Uncle Theo looked at his sister Leah. "Did you know about this?"

"No, I didn't." Aunt Leah stood up and looked down at Rita. "Don't think for one damn minute that I won't challenge this slick move."

"Me, too," Uncle Albert said. "I've got my lawyer on speed dial, girl."

"Yes, we all know how much you like to sue other folks, Uncle Albert," Rita said. She stood to face her aunt. "

"Well, you pulled off a slick move," Aunt Leah hissed.

Azalei stepped between them. "Let's not fight, mama. Rita is going to be fair to us all I'm sure."

"Huh?" Aunt Leah looked at her daughter in shock.

"Trust me," Azalei said quietly. "Rita and I discussed these arrangements. We'll get a loan to help our business, and the rest of the assets will be managed wisely. Mr. Martin drew up the trust with protections." She raised an eyebrow as some sort of signal to her mother.

Aunt Leah calmed down, but only a little. She shot a warning look at Rita. "We'll see."

"See hell." Uncle Theo pointed at Martin. "I'd like to take a look at those papers. You, hand 'em over."

"Uncle Theo, Monmon Odette's lawyer has done a

very good job making all of the necessary legal arrangements. We'll be happy to discuss the details. That's why I called this meeting," Rita crossed her arms.

"You called this meeting?" LaShaun glanced at her grandmother. "Monmon Odette."

"Rita suggested a family meeting to have my lawyer explain the particulars of how I want my estate passed on." Monmon Odette wore a smile. Her dark Creole eyes twinkled.

"Which is exactly what Mr. Martin did. Monmon's lawyer has everything nice and legal. Right, Monmon?" Rita wore a satisfied expression as she faced her fuming relatives.

"I'm sure you think so, except he's not my lawyer." Monmon Odette sipped from her cup.

Rita shook her head slowly, and wore a sad smile. "See, LaShaun. Monmon Odette gets confused sometimes. That's all right, I'll take care of everything."

"Excuse me." Savannah Honoré stood in the door. Her appearance made more than a few jaws drop. She wore a slight frown. "Sorry to get here late, Mrs. Rousselle. You did say nine thirty, right?"

"Good morning, child. You're right on time. Get up, Azalei, and let Savannah sit down." Monmon Odette pushed Azalei from her seat and gestured to Savannah. "Come sit next to me. LaShaun will get you a cup of coffee."

LaShaun leaned down, and whispered. "What are you up to, and why is she here?"

"Don't be rude by whispering around others, LaShaun." Monmon Odette sat straight. She smiled as

Savannah sat down on the antique settee next to her chair. "LaShaun wants to know what's going on, and why Savannah is here. I'm sure that's a burning question the rest of you have as well, heh?"

"This is a family meeting. Outsiders shouldn't be hearing our business, Monmon." Rita gave the newcomer a stony look. "Now you see why I needed to take control. I knew Monmon was incompetent, but this is beyond crazy. A St. Julien of all people."

"Someone should be in control, but don't count on it being you for long," Uncle Albert shot back.

"Bring it on, Uncle Albert," Rita said calmly. She turned to Savannah. "I'm my grandmother's guardian. I don't care why you're here, but it's time to leave."

"Rita, sit down and listen." Monmon Odette's sharp tone made the others snapped to attention.

"You don't seem to understand, grandmother. Our lawyer will explain it too you later. I'm in charge now." Rita's cold expression seemed triumphant.

"No, *you* don't understand. Mr. Martin is not my lawyer. Mrs. Honoré is my lawyer, and we've drafted a new trust and will." Monmon Odette's voice grew stronger as she spoke. "By the way, that power of attorney has been revoked. My lawyer will show you the order."

Chapter 4

"Your lawyer?" LaShaun and Rita blurted out in unison.

"That's ridiculous," Rita shouted.

"Calm down," Devin Martin said to Rita. He looked ruffled, but worked to keep his cool.

"Yeah, you tried to run a game, but Mama figure you out fast," Uncle Albert said pointing a stubby forefinger at Rita.

"Shut up," Rita snapped back.

"Don't tell my daddy to shut up," one Uncle Albert's daughters shouted over his shoulder. "You lookin' to get a good ass-whippin'."

"Stop hiding behind your daddy and step up then," Azalei replied, standing next to Rita.

"I think we can discuss these matters in a more civil way." Martin blinked hard when a shoving match broke out to his left between arguing cousins.

Savannah stood behind Monmon Odette's chair. She signaled to LaShaun. "Can't you settle these folks down?"

"Me? I'm still in shock over my grandmother hiring you as her attorney." LaShaun stared at Savannah. "Our families have been feuding for longer than we've been alive."

"I was--" Savannah's eye went wide as she looked past LaShaun.

LaShaun followed her gaze. One cousin had grabbed another one around the collar and was shaking him. "Damn. Help me get my grandmother out of here."

"I'm just fine. I don't want to miss a minute of this.

Most excitement I've had in a long time." Monmon Odette waved away LaShaun's attempt to help her out of the chair.

"Monmon Odette, you started this mess. Now fix it." LaShaun stared at her grandmother.

"What we need is a SWAT team," Savannah muttered. She took out her smart phone and dialed 911.

Monmon Odette stood suddenly startling LaShaun and Savannah. "Don't y'all want to know the terms of my new will?"

Her voice cracked through the clamor. Everyone looked at Monmon Odette. She sat down again with a grunt. "I thought so. Savannah, give them the particulars."

Savannah leaned down to her. "I'm not sure this is the best time."

"Yes it is. Go on." Monmon Odette nodded.

"Ahem, well, uh." Savannah looked at LaShaun who shrugged, so she took out her tablet device. "Basically the will specifies that LaShaun receive the house, its contents and the land surrounding it."

"Oh hell no," Azalei broke in before Savannah could go on. "This is the thanks we get after all we've done for you?"

"Keep talking, Savannah, and don't pay any mind to that irritating interruption." Monmon Odette glared at Azalei.

"LaShaun is also the trustee of the revocable living trust which includes a list of the following assets." Savannah stopped when Monmon Odette lifted a hand.

"That's all they need to know. I'm sure my children and grandchildren know everything I own down the last blade of grass, and every penny."

Monmon Odette turned to her relatives. "You'll have to find out how much is left when I'm dead, and not before. The most important thing to know is that LaShaun will make sure my wishes are carried out."

Rita pushed past Uncle Theo to stand in front of Monmon Odette. "I'm not surprised. You always put her ahead of everyone else, and especially me. Now let's see if this stands up in court. Everyone knows you're mind is going, not to mention being in poor health and on strong medications."

"Savannah?" Monmon Odette gazed back at Rita.

"I can successfully argue that you took advantage of Mrs. Rousselle while she was in a weakened state. The legal phrase is exerting undue influence. Once Mrs. Rousselle recovered mentally and physically after treatment…"

"Everybody knows that my doctors worked a miracle bringing me back to life," Monmon Odette added, and made the sign of the cross. "With power from the good Lord, of course."

"Once she recovered," Savannah continued, "Mrs. Rousselle realized she needed to make some changes."

"Well that don't sound much better than when Rita took over," Uncle Albert huffed for a few seconds. "Leah, you didn't know all this was goin' on under our noses? I thought you was supposed to be on top of things."

"Of course I didn't. Now shut up," Aunt Leah cut him off.

"But Azalei just said she wanted the best for Monmon. I'd think you all would be thrilled that she's doing so well that she could consult her own attorney and make all these plans. Sounds to me like she's doing just fine." LaShaun said, and smothered a laugh before it escaped.

Azalei walk over to face her. She jabbed a finger in LaShaun's chest. "You're not going to waltz back into town and take everything from us. We're the ones who have taken care of her, and she's not even grateful."

Rage crackled beneath LaShaun's skin like an itch. She could feel heat rising from the point of contact on her chest "You need to back away from me"

"What are you gonna do?" Azalei whispered. "I'm not a kid anymore scared to face up to you."

"You should be."

LaShaun grabbed the finger and bent it back until Azalei squeaked in agony. When Rita tried to intervene, LaShaun slapped her hard across the face. Rita spat a curse word, but before she could act, LaShaun wrapped her fingers around Rita's throat and squeezed. The rage drove LaShaun when she saw the animosity in her cousin's eyes. Devin managed to get between the two women and pry LaShaun's hand free. Rita stumbled back gasping for air. Aunt Leah pushed forward yelling at LaShaun. Another cousin grabbed her scarf and pulled her back.

"Y'all don't think we know you and Azalei are in on this deal with Rita?" The cousin screamed. "Go on, LaShaun, whip her ass. We got your back."

Hell broke loose. Kinfolks took sides with either LaShaun or Azalei and Rita. Savannah shouted that they could well destroy priceless antiques, and no one would get them. When no one listened, Savannah retreated to a corner of the room. The fighting spilled out to the long front porch and into the yard. Sirens whined closer. Moments later a Vermillion Parish

Sheriff's patrol car pulled into the yard, blue lights flashing.

Devin Martin swabbed sweat from his forehead with one shaking hand. "Thank God for the cavalry."

Deputy Broussard got out of his cruiser. He took several moments to observe the chaos then took put a handset to his mouth. Seconds later his voice boomed through a loud speaker on the roof of his cruiser.

"Everybody that hasn't settled down by the time I count to five is going to jail."

Deputy Arceneaux stepped out of a second cruiser. She was with her partner, a lanky man the color of dark chocolate. He walked past Deputy Arceneaux to stand on the edge of the front lawn with his feet wide apart. Deputy Broussard's countdown had the desired effect. Loud curses and name calling gradually died away. Two of LaShaun's male cousins got into a shoving match. Deputy Arceneaux's partner barked orders at them. When they broke apart the deputy stood between them.

"Who should I handcuff first?" he said, his voice a deep rumble. His tone indicated he didn't care which one; just that he would enjoy snapping the steel bracelets nice and tight.

"Arrest her. Me and Rita are going to press charges." Azalei pointed to LaShaun, and then rubbed a red spot on her left cheek. "She's going to pay my medical expenses, too. After she gets out of jail that is."

Monmon Odette came through the front door. She held onto a walker moving slowly. A teenaged great-grandson helped her along.

"Monmon Odette walked to the edge of the porch with careful steps while she held onto a teenage great-grandson. "I'm old and can't hear too good these days. Say again, Azalei?"

"LaShaun..." Azalei stopped when she locked gazes with her grandmother.

"Somebody wanna tell me what happened?" Deputy Broussard said.

"Family discussion that got out of hand. Nobody got hurt, and everybody is going to go home and cool off. Ain't that right, children?" Monmon Odette.

Uncle Theo cleared his throat and tucked his shirt back into his pants. "Mostly a bunch of yelling, officer. No real harm done."

"Yeah, nothin' but a little family disagreement." Uncle Albert put on a tight smile.

"So that's the story, huh?" Deputy Broussard looked around the crowd, but no one answered. Then he stared hard at LaShaun.

"Apparently we're all sticking to it." LaShaun looked at Rita and Azalei.

""Then I suggest everybody follow Miss Odette's advice and go home," Deputy Broussard said.

He nodded to the other deputies. They in turn walked into the crowd. Deputy Arceneaux and her partner herded people toward the cars parked in the driveway and on the lawn. LaShaun's two uncles, aunt, and Rita lingered on the porch. The deputies concentrated on moving the younger, more combative relatives out. When Deputy Broussard turned back to LaShaun she shrugged and walked toward him with a smile.

"Thanks so much for being a source law and order. Just what these folks needed." LaShaun titled her head to one side when he squinted at her. "What?"

"People around town said you were trouble. Looks like you're eager to prove they're right." Deputy Broussard rested a hand on one slim hip.

"What else did they say about me?"

"Isn't that enough? Not much of a character endorsement if you ask me." Deputy Broussard looked down at her with a stone face.

LaShaun felt a rush of heat beneath her skin, the sign when she "saw" clearly what others did not. Deputy Broussard had his will set on not finding her attractive. She could almost hear his thoughts, that Sheriff Triche had lost his edge and the sharp instincts that had served him well.

"You're wrong about him, the sheriff I mean," LaShaun said quietly.

Broussard's gaze narrowed like the laser on a Glock pistol. "Don't try your magic tricks on me."

"Relax, Deputy Broussard. I'm not trying to put a spell on you."

"Yeah, I'll try to remember that," he replied in a bland tone. He took sunglasses from his shirt pocket and put them on.

LaShaun became irritated with herself for even having this discussion with him. She kept her temper in check, barely. "Think what you want. You through here or you intend to search me for weapons?"

Deputy Broussard looked at her for a few seconds. "Is that an offer, ma'am?"

LaShaun studied him as the minutes ticked by, and the temperature between them rose. She then turned away and walked toward the porch. "Goodbye, Deputy."

"She didn't start any of this trouble, Deputy

Broussard," Monmon Odette called out. She was now sitting in a rocker on the porch.

"Yes, ma'am." Deputy Broussard nodded to Monmon Odette respectfully. He looked at LaShaun. "I'll see you around."

"Humph." LaShaun stood next to her grandmother.

She wanted to think of a reply with more pepper in it, but those dark Cajun eyes along with the silken soft burr of his accent threw her. His voice sounded like a pleasant promise instead of a warning from the law. Deputy Broussard's lean, muscular frame folded into the cruiser with ease. He spoke into the radio handset for several minutes before he drove off.

"Don't think this is over. Not even close," Azalei shouted. She marched to her cherry red mustang and drove off.

Rita and Devin Martin stood together speaking softly. After a few seconds, both glanced at LaShaun. Martin left first, backing his BMW down the driveway after another car behind him left.

"You may have this round, but I'm not done with you yet," Rita said to LaShaun.

"Stop listening to Aunt Leah and Azalei, Rita. They're poison times two. There's no need for us fight."

"Guess again," Rita snapped cutting her off. "That old woman always favored you over me. I got what was left once she showered you with the best. I'm not taking seconds anymore."

"So that's how it is, huh?" LaShaun squinted at her.

"Yeah, that's how it is. Don't underestimate me." Rita gave LaShaun a heated head to toe glare then strode to her car.

"Hell." LaShaun took several deep breaths to calm her nerves. She went back to the long gallery where Monmon Odette sat gently moving a cane rocking chair back and forth.

"Still glad you came back, Cher?" Monmon Odette cocked an eyebrow at her.

LaShaun turned to watch Rita's Honda Accord disappearing around the curve of the long driveway. "Home sweet home."

LYNN EMERY

Chapter 5

The next day LaShaun went into town. Three blocks into her walk down Main Street and LaShaun had an overwhelming urge to slap somebody. The stares and whispers bothered her more than she thought they would. She'd forgotten the relentless memory of small town folks. In Los Angeles she'd been just one of millions, another transplant chasing California gold in one variety or another. What LaShaun had found was a way to be herself without the claustrophobic definitions of her family's past or the judgment of others. She had changed, but Beau Chene was the same. The downtown looked like a typical tourist area in rural Louisiana. Quaint antique shops and restaurants featuring Creole cuisine made up most of the small business district. Savannah stood in the door to her father's curio and souvenir shop, arms crossed in a defensive posture.

A feud between the St. Julien and Rousselle families that crossed four generations at least was another legend in the parish. After so many years, the teenage romance between Antoine St. Julien and LaShaun's mother promised an uneasy truce. When the young Antoine fell in love with someone else, the woman who had become Savannah's mother, the feud didn't just continue. Things got nasty. Francine spiraled into self-destruction. Monmon Odette blamed Antoine, and LaShaun saw Savannah as the enemy. Yet, in her hour of need Monmon Odette had reached out to the St. Julien family.

"Hello," Savannah said. She looked into LaShaun's eyes intently as trying to detect some sign of trouble to come. "So I'm guessing you want to find out why your grandmother hired a St. Julien to be her lawyer."

LaShaun let out a long sigh. "Hello to you, too, Savannah. We're gonna skip the small talk I guess."

"No sense wasting time being phony. So, what's the deal, LaShaun? You wanna start a riot in town, too?"

"Well at least you have a sense of humor these days."

"Not seeing you for ten years helped," Savannah shot back.

"I'm back to visit my grandmother. This may be my last chance to spend time with her," LaShaun replied quietly.

Savannah's expression softened a little. "Of course. So you must have plenty of questions about this dramatic peace treaty between the St. Julien family and your grandmother."

"You betcha I do," LaShaun said and shook her head.

"Come over to my office. It's on the other side of the building." Savannah turned back and waved to two employees in the shop. Then she led the way to the south side of the building. Gold letters on a glass window had her name and "Attorney" under it. They went into the small lobby. A young man was on the phone.

"That's Jarius. He's my part-time paralegal, and full-time criminal justice student. Mostly he's a student." Savannah waved to him. She went into her office then shut the door when LaShaun followed. "Let's start with the biggest mystery I guess, why Mrs. Rousselle would call me of all people."

"I'm all ears." LaShaun sat down in a dark red leather chair opposite its twin in front of Savannah's desk.

Savannah laughed and sat down next to her. "Actually she called my daddy."

LaShaun fell back in the chair. "This just keeps getting stranger."

"I know, I know. When she called, I actually begged him not to go see her. He told me to stop being silly. Daddy always thought that talk of her being a voodoo woman was a bunch of nonsense."

"You didn't. I used to really creep you out." LaShaun started to smile at the memory of her childhood antics. But, she stopped. "I'm really sorry about all that."

"Gee, thanks. Scaring me into nightmares is really amusing," Savannah shot back. Then she sighed and shrugged. "But that was a long time ago."

"And the Claude Trosclair murder?" LaShaun studied her closely.

"Okay, I'll admit it. I thought you were at least in on it at first. But the investigation didn't produce any credible evidence to support that you were involved." Savannah used lawyer speak.

"So you're not completely convinced I'm innocent," LaShaun replied.

"Oh I know you're not *innocent*," Savannah said with a snort. "But I don't think you killed him. And by the way, slapping around your kinfolk is not the way to prove you've changed."

"They provoked me, especially that loud-mouthed Azalei." LaShaun frowned then looked at Savannah. "Which brings me back to you representing Monmon."

"Daddy and Miss Odette talked a long time, not sure when. I don't know what they discussed either, he wouldn't say. Just came in one day, and said she needed my help. The next day he brought her to my office, and she apologized for causing me any pain. We talked about my mother, and how Miss Odette took her grief out on us for all the wrong reasons."

"I can't take much more of these shocks to the system, girl." LaShaun placed a hand on her chest.

"I was pretty damn near speechless myself. Thing is my father acted like it was no big deal." Savannah shook her head. "Anyway, your grandmother wanted to be back in control. Once she got stronger, Rita made it clear that she didn't plan to give up power of attorney. "

"My grandmother probably didn't like that much," LaShaun said.

"Now that is an understatement. But, she didn't make a big fuss. She just quietly planned to deal with her 'problem'. First, she called my daddy. Then she hired me. We got an order from court to force Rita to disclose financial records two weeks ago. We think money was withdrawn from one, maybe two, of her investment accounts."

LaShaun stood up. "I'm going to talk to Rita right now. If she thinks I'm going to just sit around while she steals from her own grandmother…" She went to the lobby.

"That's a bad idea. We've had enough Rousselle family drama." Savannah followed her. "LaShaun, let's arrange a meeting with Rita and Devin Martin."

"Uh-huh, this calls for some straight talk woman to woman, family to family." LaShaun went through the front door, but Savannah's hand on her arm stopped her.

"Don't track Rita down while you're fired up," Savannah said in a level tone.

LaShaun shook her head and let out a long slow breath to calm down. "Which might be exactly what Rita, Azalei and my aunt want me to do."

"They'll use anything you do as evidence you're not morally fit to manage the trust." Savannah lightly tapped the screen of her tablet computer and a list of contacts appeared. The she dialed his number on her desk phone. She hit a button as the phone rang. After a brief time, an office assistant put them through. "Hello, Devin. I have you on speaker. LaShaun Rousselle is in my office."

After a moment of hesitation Martin spoke. "Hello, ladies. What can I do for you today?"

"We need to talk about some discrepancies in Mrs. Rousselle's accounts. We should arrange for a meeting. I've hired a forensic accountant."

"Wait, I have another call coming through. Hold for a second. Sorry about that, but this won't take long." Then he was gone, and easy listening jazz replaced his voice.

"How much you want to bet they're in his office right now cooking up a scheme?" LaShaun's temper came to a boil again.

"I wouldn't doubt it after that explosion yesterday." Savannah was about to go on when the music stopped.

"Sorry again. Listen, I'm tied up right now on another matter. I'll consult my client and get back to you."

"I hope we hear from you soon so we can get any

misunderstanding resolved." Savannah made a face as though she already knew the answer of where the money went.

"Of course. I'll be in touch. Have a great day, ladies." Martin rang off.

"We'll give them some time. If I don't hear from them in the next two days, we'll talk about what to do next." Savannah stared at LaShaun. "And it won't involve a knock down drama fest. Right?"

"Right," LaShaun said. Her fiery Rousselle nature would just have to cool it. For now the slow wheels of the legal system would have to be her way of dealing with Rita and Azalei.

Savannah walked out of the office with her. "I know you want answers yesterday, but at least they can't get at more of the money."

"True. Now they know we know." LaShaun squinted for a few seconds before she put on her sunglasses.

"We're talking about possible criminal charges if what we suspect is true. A great reason they might decide not to challenge the trust and the will," Savannah said.

Deputy Broussard drove up. One brawny arm rested in the window of the cruiser.. His sunglasses, strong jaw, and uniform caused female heads of all ages to turn for a second, even a third look. He nodded to Savannah but stared at LaShaun.

"Good afternoon, Miss Savannah. Are you all right?"

Savannah gazed at him then at LaShaun. "Hi. I'm fine, and you?"

"Can't complain much. I'm just out and about

keepin' an eye on things." Deputy Broussard nodded. "Ms. Rousselle."

"You think folks need protection from me?" LaShaun said.

"Well based on that brawl and your reputation, keeping an eye on your might not be a bad idea." Deputy Broussard gazed at LaShaun. His lips curve up in a brief smile that he suppressed quickly.

"I'm going to complain about police harassment if this keeps up, Deputy Broussard," LaShaun said and crossed her arms.

"No ma'am. I have the best of intentions."

"Uh-huh."

LaShaun tried to feel annoyed, or at least indifferent. But the dark brown hair curled just to the edge of his shirt collar made him look too appealing. Not to mention she enjoyed the way his lips moved when he talked in that soft Cajun accent.

"Y'all excuse me. LaShaun, remember what I said." Savannah looked at the deputy. She passed close to LaShaun on her way into the office. "Stay out of trouble."

"I'm going to be so low key you won't know I'm in town." LaShaun grinned when Savannah rolled her eyes and walked into her office.

"That was some family reunion y'all had the other day. You might wanna listen to your lawyer, and save the battles for civil court."

The dark lenses hid any message she might read in his eyes. LaShaun walked closer to the car. "That's your friendly advice to keep me out of trouble?"

"Yes, ma'am. I'm being friendly." He pulled the glasses down for a second then pushed them back up. "I hope to see you again, and not on a disturbance call either."

With one last tempting smile, he waved goodbye, and eased the cruiser away from the curb. Other cars promptly slowed down to match his speed. LaShaun looked around to find several of the locals staring at her with interest. No doubt her little "friendly" chat with the hunky deputy would give them plenty to talk about for the rest of the day. LaShaun was about to leave when a snow white Lexus SUV pulled up to the curb exactly where the deputy's cruiser had been moments before.

Quentin Trosclair sat behind the wheel. He'd been her lover and fellow suspect in the murder of his rich, mean as a snake grandfather. She had to admit the nasty piece of work had aged gracefully. Quentin looked fit and trim. Dressed in a light yellow knit shirt and khaki pants, he was still handsome in a spoiled, decadent kind of way. His black hair cut short.

"Well, well. Returning to the scene of the crime," he said.

"Being home is getting to be more fun by the day." LaShaun tapped her right fist against one jean clad thigh as she gazed back at Quentin.

Quentin seemed confident that LaShaun would wait stay put to talk to him. He removed his designer sunglasses to reveal those mesmerizing blue eyes. Dozens of southern debutantes had fallen prey to his sparkling smile, a lure into danger. Yet, LaShaun also saw the thin lines around his mouth and a few that framed his eyes. She knew those not only came from the passage of time. Greed and cruelty could twist his handsome face into something terrible to see.

"Looking good as always," Quentin said, his gaze sliding down her body then back up to her face.

LaShaun walked closer to the Lexus. She noticed the gold band on the ring finger of his left hand. "Congratulations on your recent marriage."

"How did you know? Oh, but of course. You're the mysterious, supernatural LaShaun Rousselle." His voice dropped to a melodramatic deep tone. Then he grinned at her.

In spite of the danger in that perfect rich boy smile LaShaun smiled back. "Naturally."

"Maybe you've been keeping up with news about me because you care." Quentin leaned a bit out of the window toward her.

"You still have a rich fantasy life," LaShaun looked away from his intent gaze.

"Always when I see you," Quentin replied. He pursed his lips then relaxed against the seat back. "How's Miss Odette? Better I hope."

"Well as can be expected. Thanks."

LaShaun realized they were the center of attention. Mr. Thibodeaux, the owner of an upholstery shop, moved a broom around on the sidewalk. His attention was on LaShaun and Quentin. Several other shop owners seemed to have discovered outdoor tasks that needed doing as well. Cars slowed, tongues wagged and eyebrows raised.

"Hop in and let me take you for a ride," Quentin said as he patted the soft leather passenger seat beside him.

"I can think of a whole list of reasons why that's a bad idea." LaShaun said. "Your wife probably already knows we're talking."

"Our marriage is built on trust," Quentin said. His dark eyes sparkled with amusement.

"Then she's not too bright, or else she's from out of town," LaShaun said with a laugh.

Quentin laughed. "Both. Meredith is a sweet girl from a fine family with deep roots in Vicksburg, Mississippi."

"Well hush my mouth." LaShaun put a hand over her heart like a southern belle. "Surely they have CNN in Vicksburg."

"Yes indeed. They also follow the financial news." Quentin nodded.

The Trosclair name and wealth still counted for a lot, especially with the old southern families. Besides, she knew very well that Quentin had enough bad boy charm to melt the polar ice caps. With all his assets LaShaun knew more than a few old southern families would be happy to believe in his innocence.

"Now don't tell me you're afraid of what people might think," Quentin goaded.

"Like my reputation could get much worse around here," LaShaun replied with sharp laugh.

"Exactly. So you don't have anything to lose. Surely you're not scared of me." Quentin raised one dark eyebrow at her.

"I'm more selective about the company I keep these days."

He put his sunglasses back on. "Really? I hear a certain deputy has taken an interest in you. Boring and broke is your type these days I suppose."

"You don't really think I'd hook up with a cop?" LaShaun laughed. What she really wanted was to throw Quentin off. He had a mean streak, and might go after

Broussard just to prove a point to LaShaun.

"Yeah, does sound kinda silly. If he's bothering you just let me know, darlin'." Quentin nodded.

LaShaun sighed. "I don't believe for a second you control anyone, especially not the sheriff. He'd still like to lock you up before he leaves office."

"In his dreams. That old man will retire in another six months. Hopefully we'll have a fresh blood and a new perspective."

"You're backing a candidate?"

"I'm not into politics." Quentin smiled back at her.

"Right." LaShaun looked at him. The Trosclairs didn't run for office, but they were more than happy to control the people elected.

"Triche could stay in office until he keeled over, and he'd never have evidence against me."

"I don't know. Forensic science has made a lot of advances in the past ten years. Maybe one of the candidates for his job might take an interest."

"Has that Broussard guy said something to you?" Quentin took off his sunglasses to gaze at her intently.

"Not really, but coming up with new evidence on a famous cold case might definitely help anybody win the top cop job." LaShaun shrugged.

Quentin snorted. "Broussard doesn't have a chance. He isn't as smart as he thinks he is. Besides, Brad Gautreau is a tough opponent."

"I met him. He's a jerk," LaShaun replied.

"I heard you two didn't hit it off at the station the other night."

"So you're chummy with the jerk; birds of a feather." LaShaun began to get a clear picture, and it left a sour taste in her mouth.

"Say the word, and he won't be a problem for you either." Quentin shrugged. "Sure you don't want to share a something delicious with me? I know a wonderful place we can go."

"Sitting across from you would spoil my appetite."

"I wasn't talking about having a meal, baby." Quentin ran the tip of his tongue around his lips and made a smacking sound.

"You really overestimate your own charm." LaShaun gave a grunt of disgust.

As she walked away from the Lexus her skin tingled. Her affair with Quentin had been an adrenaline rush times ten. He'd satisfied her need for breaking all the rules. Like an addict, she'd never be entirely free of the craving. Something pulled at her, some force. A whispering call came from somewhere. Was it the wind or inside her head? The tingle became an itch to turn around, and go after Quentin. Trembling, she crossed her arms to ward off a chill even the intense Louisiana sunshine couldn't stop. She closed her eyes for a second, and said a prayer. This was no ordinary urge. The loa had grown stronger. But so had she, stronger in her faith. With a deep breath, she pushed back hard. The sensation subsided.

Quentin flashed a wicked grin at her as he drove past. "Ask your cousin Rita why you'll be seeing more of me."

"What?" LaShaun spun around with a gasp, but the Lexus picked up speed. Quentin waved a hand before closing the car window and gunning the engine.

Chapter 6

For the next two days, LaShaun ignored Savannah's advice. She tried to call Rita on the phone repeatedly. All she got for her trouble was the recording of Rita's voice telling her to leave a message. After twelve messages LaShaun wanted to break something when she heard recorded greeting. Savannah told her that Martin kept putting her off, saying that he wasn't able to get in touch with Rita. When LaShaun told Savannah she thought he was a lying scumbag, Savannah again cautioned her against rash action. LaShaun's response was to drive out to Rita's townhouse and pound on the front door. No answer. LaShaun went back to her SUV to sit and wait, determined to catch Rita coming or going.

"You got a good reason for bein' here, ma'am?"

LaShaun jumped at the deep voice outside her car window. Deputy Gautreau lifted an eyebrow at her. He tapped on the window. LaShaun hit the button to open the window.

"Visiting a relative," LaShaun replied with a smile. "I don't see a 'No Parking' sign either. But it's reassuring to know you're on patrol, deputy."

"I got a call about a possible disturbance," he replied.

"This is such a quiet, nice neighborhood. The only noise I've heard is birds singing." LaShaun waved a hand at the landscaped lawns. "

"Uh-huh. Be careful on your way home. Winding country roads can be real tricky."

"Thanks for your concern."

He flashed an artificial smile, but didn't make a move to leave. His stone cold gaze seemed to indicate he would stay put as long as she did. LaShaun started the SUV and drove off. She glanced in rear view mirror expecting to see him following her, but he was gone.

When she got home, Savannah was just pulling up in her car. Monmon Odette rocked on the front porch humming. LaShaun was worried about her. She seemed in another world, strangely disconnected from everything. After checking to make sure she didn't need anything, LaShaun and Savannah went into the living room.

"Martin claims he can't get in touch with Rita. I tried tracking down Azalei, and she's gone underground as well. I spoke to the forensic accountant again. She finished her examination. Two accounts have been cleaned out, about two hundred and fifty thousand dollars."

"Those conniving scam artists," LaShaun said.

"It gets worse. Rita took out s second mortgage on your grandmother's house, and the payments are behind three months. The home health care agency hasn't been paid in three months, but luckily, they decided to switch from private pay to Medicare billing. Even so there's a big balance. I'm afraid your grandmother's available cash accounts might be stretched to the limit. I've contacted the bank. If we scramble we just might avoid foreclosure."

For another hour, LaShaun discussed options with Savannah. The accountant had recommendations. LaShaun had little time to digest it all because the creditors wanted answers yesterday. Not to mention the IRS and Louisiana Department of Revenue had questions about taxes due on the withdrawals from the investment accounts. By the time Savannah left LaShaun felt drained of energy. She didn't know which was more intense, her need to cry or beat the hell out of someone.

She didn't even consider talking to Monmon Odette. For the first time LaShaun understood. Her grandmother was showing signs of dementia. No wonder the once razor sharp mind hadn't seen through the schemes being perpetrated on her. LaShaun spent the rest of the afternoon taking care of her.

The next day Sheriff Triche and Deputy Gautreau showed up. When Deputy Broussard followed a few minutes later, he and Gautreau exchanged decidedly unfriendly glances. The three men wore grim faces as she led them into the living room.

"Afternoon, LaShaun." Sheriff Triche looked tired. His face flushed red.

"I have a feeling the three of you didn't drive out here to chat about the weather." LaShaun didn't like the way Gautreau glared at her. "Isn't anybody out chasing criminals? The entire department seems to be on my doorstep."

"We didn't plan on Broussard showing up," Gautreau drawled. "Wonder why?"

"Not now," Sheriff Triche snapped. "Your cousin Azalei is missing, at least according to her mama. She seems to think you know something about it."

"Azalei and I have never been close," LaShaun replied. She laughed. "Trust me, we haven't been doing lunch."

"No, you've been too busy trading punches and threatening her," Gautreau put in. He was about to go on when Aunt Leah made a dramatic entrance.

"Get her to talk. She's done something to my child. She's not answering her cell phone, and I haven't been able to find her for three days. Nobody has seen her." Aunt Leah pointed at LaShaun. "You tell me what you did to Azalei."

"Thanks for calling the Sheriff, Aunt Leah. This visit saves me a trip into town to press charges against your baby girl."

"She wouldn't leave without telling me." Aunt Leah's voice cracked. She wore a frantic expression. She spun to face Sheriff Triche. "I'm telling you something is wrong. All of her clothes are still in her apartment. Now who runs off like that?"

"A scheming thief who just stole a lot of money from her sick grandmother, that's who," LaShaun put in.

"You're nothing but a liar." Aunt Leah took a step toward LaShaun

LaShaun looked at Sheriff Triche. "This is all an act to give Azalei more time to get away."

"You've been nothing but poison since the day you were born," Aunt Leah said.

"Just calm down and go on home." Sheriff Triche took her by the elbow and led her out. Moments later he came back. "If you hear from either of them call me."

"If you hear anything from them, don't do anything crazy. Let me know first," Broussard said to LaShaun.

Gautreau grunted. "You hear that, Sheriff?"

"You call *me* if you hear from your cousins, LaShaun. Let's go," Sheriff Triche clipped the command to his two deputies.

Chase hesitated and started to speak, but look in his

boss's eyes stopped him. The two younger men march out ahead of the Sheriff. When they were gone, LaShaun locked the door and turned to find her grandmother in the hallway panting with the exertion of taking each step.

"You should be in bed." LaShaun went to her quickly

"You escaped the madness, and now because of me you're pulled back in. Perhaps I should have let them have it all. Then just watch them claw each other to death over it."

LaShaun put an arm around her shoulder. "This kind of commotion is the last thing you need. Everything is just fine. I'll get you settled, and then we'll both have a cup of chamomile."

"Evil has come back to tempt you, child. You must fight it. I'll show you how." Monmon clutched LaShaun's hand."

"You need rest," LaShaun said.

"Soon I will find eternal rest, if the good Lord forgives my sins. Now listen to me press the inlaid panel of the old desk in the salon. Obey your grandmother, girl. Go." Monmon Odette pushed LaShaun toward the polished teakwood desk against the far wall.

"First sit down." LaShaun helped her to one of the chairs in the living room. Then she went to the desk.

LaShaun studied the panel just above the flat writing surface. A lighter shade of wood inset was a beautiful contrast to the polished teakwood. She pressed it with her fingertips and a section slid out smoothly. A black velvet pouch was in the center next to an envelope yellowed by age.

"You see it, oui? Bring the pouch here." Monmon Odette beckoned to her.

LaShaun picked it up. Several other objects were in the hidden compartment, but she was immediately distracted. Whatever was in the pouch, it seemed to grow warmer the longer she held it. She crossed back to Monmon Odette and handed it to her. Her grandmother whispered so low that LaShaun couldn't make out the words. Monmon Odette tugged both ends of the drawstring, and emptied the pouch into her lap. Four gemstones and two pendants came out. One of the pendants was on a silver chain, the other on a leather cord. The gems glittered as though lit from within.

"Ah, these are wonderful, child. Now listen carefully. The crystals are rose quartz, amethyst, clear quartz and citrine. Make a pendant or bracelet with these to protect your children."

"What children?" LaShaun said with a laugh.

Monmon Odette looked up at her. "You will have children, and they must be protected. As much as a mother can do." Then she looked back down the gemstones. "Nothing is certain if they stray too far. I learned that with your mama, and Rita's daddy. They were wild, and didn't listen to the wisdom of elders. Ah, well. Neither did when I was young."

"You did your best, Monmon."

"Hmm, I pray Le Bon Dieu finds it so." Monmon Odette sighed. "But you will have children, more than one. I'm not sure how many though."

"I'll need to find a man first, don't you think?" LaShaun smiled at her with affection.

"Speaking of that, this will guard your loved one. Give it to him." Monmon Odette held up the pendant on a leather cord.

LaShaun took it to the window to get a better looked. A large piece of black onyx formed a circle. In the center of the onyx was a sterling silver circle carved with a howling wolf's head and feathers on either side. A lapis lazuli gemstone sat just below the wolf head between the feathers.

"This is beautiful."

"The wolf is a symbol of power. Lapis lazuli provides good luck, and black onyx provides spiritual protection." Monmon Odette nodded.

"When I find a good man I'll be sure he gets this." LaShaun walked back to her grandmother.

"He's closer than you think, Cher." Monmon Odette looked at her with a twinkle in her eye.

"If he is I haven't seen him," LaShaun quipped.

Her grandmother chuckled softly. "You will when you open your eyes. Now this is for you. Green aventurine set against back onyx for wealth and power. You'll need this to hold onto my money."

Monmon Odette smiled her approval when LaShaun put the silver chain around her neck that held the second amulet. Then she put the gems and wolf amulet back into the pouch.

LaShaun sat on the small ottoman near Monmon Odette that matched the sofa and chairs in the room."Thank you, sweet grandmother. What other secrets do you have to reveal?"

"Read the old journals I will give you. Those hold a lot of family history." Monmon Odette fell silent for a few moments. Then she took one of LaShaun's hands in both of hers. "But remember to pray for strength against the evil that tempts you. For many years, I thought the power passed to me could overcome any obstacle. Certainly, no man would control me, and no spirit frightened me. I had to learn many hard lessons."

"Yes, Monmon." LaShaun gazed at the solemn expression her grandmother wore.

Monmon Odette smiled as though to banish the clouds that her words had brought. "Ah, but you are young and lovely. And the day is bright with sunshine. No more gloomy talk. Here is Tasha, on time as usual. Get out of the house."

"But I need to prepare your lunch, and change the linens." LaShaun shook her head. She went to the front door, opened the lock and the door.

"Hello there. How you feelin' today Miz Odette?" Tasha grinned at them both.

"Doing okay for an old, old lady," Monmon Odette smiled back at her.

"Glad to hear it. I'm going to get set up so we can do your exercises. First, I'm going to change your linens, take a look at your medicines to make sure we got the latest changes from the nurse and then we'll get started. Then you'll have a nice relaxing warm shower." She bustled off humming to herself.

"See? I'm going to be tied up with Miss Bumble Bee buzzing around for the next few hours. Go on out and enjoy yourself." Monmon Odette pushed against LaShaun to press her point.

"Okay, okay. No need to shove me out the door." LaShaun laughed. "Seems like those exercises are working."

"Bunch of nuisance nonsense if you ask me," Monmon Odette grumbled.

LaShaun made sure Monmon Odette didn't need

her, and Tasha had everything under control. Only then did she take her grandmother's advice. Grabbing her keys from the kitchen counter LaShaun decided to go for a drive.

She followed Rousselle Lane until it intersected with the larger street. Only two narrow lanes and not much bigger than Rousselle Road, Bayou Rouge Road had only been paved for two decades. Palmettos and other thick vegetation came right up to the edges of the black top. To clear her head LaShaun drove with the windows down. Instead of keeping strait to Teche Bayou that lay on the edge of Rousselle family property, she turned south. Ten minutes later, she arrived at Bayou Rouge, a smaller body of water that flowed into Teche Lake six miles to the west.

This used to be her favorite getaway spot when she was in trouble with her grandmother. She parked on a grassy slope. Once out of the SUV LaShaun followed a dirt path down to the water. A breeze brought a little relief from the hot noonday sun. Cattle egrets and herons perched around the far shore. Sunlight sparkled on parts of the water like tiny crystals. The soothing sounds of insects, birds, and wind in the leaves soothed away the tension from her body.

Her mind free, LaShaun thought about the "thing" that had taken control of her back at Monmon's house. Years ago her wild ways had awakened more wickedness that LaShaun had been prepared to embrace. And now it was back, and just as hungry to possess her. She'd known the risks, but couldn't bear to stay away. Not when she might never see her grandmother alive again. Monmon Odette could help her, but she was weak. Such an effort would kill her.

Besides, LaShaun had no right to ask that of her grandmother. She would find a way to deal with this force on her own. She had no choice. LaShaun fingered the amulet around her neck. Then she took the onyx and silver wolf's head amulet from the pocket in her shirt. The stone felt warm in her hand. In the past she had allowed envy, resentment, and even lust to rule in her heart. Had she changed so much? If she had then no spirit should be able to influence her so easily. Deep in thought, LaShaun didn't realize she wasn't alone until it was too late.

"Hey, baby. How you doin' today? Now we can really get this party started."

Two men, each holding a can of beer, approached squinting against the bright sunshine. Grime and the sun had darkened their otherwise white skin. One of the men tried to put on a charming smile. The effort only made him look sinister

"Hi you doin', darlin'? Out enjoying the day like us, I see. My names is-- "

"Bob, that's his name. I'm John," his friend cut him off. He was a short man with a beard and mustache. He had on a plaid shirt with the sleeves pushed up to the elbow.

"Bob and John, huh?" LaShaun faced them with her arms down to her side. A tingle up her spine signaled this was a bad development.

"We've got cold beer and sandwiches. Even got us a CD player with funky music." The one called "Bob" stared at LaShaun's breasts.

"No thanks. I'm on my way home." LaShaun took a step back. John circled to her left in a move that blocked her escape route. "Look, guys, I'm not looking for a party or company.

"Bein' all by yourself ain't no fun, girl." Bob walked close to her and stroked her arm.

LaShaun slapped his hand hard enough to rock Bob's entire body. "You don't want to mess with me."

"I like 'em wild," John crowed.

"Let's see how much fire you got, girl," Bob said.

He came in close again reaching for LaShaun breast. What he got was a fist to his groin and pain. Bob doubled over with a yelp. His buddy laughed as he grabbed LaShaun from behind and ground his pelvis against her.

"Looks like it's just you and me. My friend can't do you any good in the lovin' department." John tried to put his hand under LaShaun's t-shirt.

"Get off me."

LaShaun struggled to get free. John laughed again, but stopped when she jammed a heel into the top of his foot. John grunted but his boot took most of the impact, and he t held on. Bob still lay in the thick grass, both hands cupping his privates. With all the force she had left, LaShaun fought back. Seconds seemed like hours as the man managed to force her to one knee onto the ground. She screamed, but they were in the middle of bayou country. No other boaters or fishers were within sight. Bob put a grimy hand over her mouth. LaShaun twisted her head until she could bite into the flesh below his thumb.

"Damn bitch," Bob shouted. He gripped her harder. "Now you really owe me a good time."

His pal tried to get up, but winced and sank down again. He swiped sweat from his eyes. "Get her good for me, too."

Bob grabbed a handful of LaShaun's hair and yanked. But she didn't feel the pain. Instead, a ball of rage lodged in her chest like a hot chunk of coal. LaShaun focused on the image of the rock as it began to glow red around the edges. The scent of smoke filled her nostrils, and her focus narrowed until the scenery around her disappeared.

The burly man hissed in agony and let go of LaShaun. He stared at the palm of his hand. "What the hell? She burned me like a hot poker."

"Don't be stupid." His friend seemed to have recovered. He stood. "We're not leavin' here until she pays for being such a hellcat."

"Uh-uh, Jerry. Somethin' ain't right with this woman. I say we haul ass outta here."

"Fool, you just told her my real name." Jerry turned to LaShaun with a nasty smile. "Now you really gotta a problem, baby."

The unmistakable earsplitting crack of a pump action shotgun made them all freeze. Deputy Broussard emerged from the brush nearby dressed in jeans and an army green shirt. "Don't move fellas."

"We just havin' a good time on the bayou is all." Jerry spread his arms wide out as though showing the man he was no threat.

"Just hangin' out fishin' and stuff. We got some beer and music. You can join us. Here you go." The other man started toward the dropped six-pack.

"I said don't move," Chase replied. "You make me nervous when you start jumping around like that. I might think you mean me some harm."

"Just stay calm, man. No need for that shotgun now. We're all friends out here." The man that called himself "Bob" tried a smile. His left eye twitched when Chase swung the barrel in his direction.

"I'm having a hard time believing the lady considers you boys her *friends*. You okay?" Chase asked without taking his eyes off the two men.

LaShaun brushed dirt from her jeans and blouse. "Yeah. I've got a whole list of names for these two, and friends ain't one of 'em."

"You gentlemen will be going to jail so we can sort this out. I'm Deputy Broussard, Vermillion Parish Sheriff's Department. My badge is my left back pocket," Chase said to LaShaun.

She stared at his butt, shown to great advantage in the well-fitted blue jeans. LaShaun raised an eyebrow at him, but he continued to focus on the two men. Using the tips of her fingers, LaShaun slid his wallet from the back pocket. She flipped it open to show his badge. She looked at the driver's license opposite it. Chase wore a crooked grin in the photo, and a lock of his black hair was across the right side of his forehead.

"You boys got more trouble than you bargained for today," LaShaun murmured, but continued to gaze at handsome picture.

Chase glanced at her briefly. "Turn around. I have some rope in my tackle box back on the ground there. We're gonna tie them up until I can get the plastic cuffs from my truck."

"Oh, now wait a minute, buddy." Bob looked at his companion.

"Deputy Broussard," Chase snapped back at him.

"Listen, how 'bout we apologize to the lady and just let bygones be bygones. We saw a pretty woman and got a little too flirty is all." Jerry rubbed his jaw nervously. "We're real sorry, ma'am. Ain't we, Wally?"

"Yeah, yeah," Wally nodded with fervor.

"We made a few sassy remarks, but that was all. You know how it is with us guys, buddy. I mean Deputy Broussard."

Before LaShaun could speak, Chase replied in a voice cold and hard as steel. "She scratches on her wrists and her clothes were messed up."

"Let 'em go, Deputy Broussard." LaShaun smiled at the men, causing them to look even more worried.

"Are you sure?" Chase frowned.

"I don't need the hassle of pressing charges. At least not this time." LaShaun brushed more dirt from her jeans.

"I wrote down the plate number on that raggedy blue truck of yours. It'll take me maybe five minutes to find out everything about you two, right down to what you had for breakfast this morning. You get what I'm sayin'?" Chase lowered the shotgun a bit.

"Yes, sir," Wally muttered, a sullen expression stamped on his scruffy face.

He bumped into his friend as they both left quickly, first at a trot that turned into a full run through the thick underbrush. When they disappeared. Chase lowered the shotgun until it pointed at the ground. LaShaun let out the deep breath that she'd been holding.

"Maybe you should go to the hospital and get checked out." Chase gave her swift once over like seasoned lawman trained to pick up details.

"I'm okay. Thanks for coming to the rescue again." LaShaun started to shiver. She folded her arms in an attempt to regain control.

Chase looked around quickly then rested the shotgun against a tree trunk nearby. He wrapped one muscular arm around her. "They're gone. The way they took off outta here, they may be ten miles down the road by now. Between the two of us, we scared the spit outta of 'em. You're safe."

LaShaun could only shake her head. After about a minute she could feel his solid presence calm the trembling sensation that had taken over her. "Are hugs part of your deputy training?"

"Right there in section five of the lawman's handbook." Chase smiled at her. Then he stepped back and picked up his shotgun again. "At least let me put some antiseptic on those scratches."

"I'll survive." LaShaun rubbed her arms to get rid of the last bit of tension.

"Okay you've proven to me you're tough. Now how about showing me you've got some sense? Brushing the grass and dirt off those won't stop infection."

LaShaun looked at the smears of dirt on her forearms. "Guess you've got a point."

Chase nodded for her to follow him. He led the way back through the woods away from the bayou. "Take me to my truck, and you can follow me."

LaShaun walked behind him, but she kept looking over her shoulder and around. The encounter with the two men had frightened LaShaun more than she cared to admit. She wanted to tough it out, to tell him she could leave on her own. The truth was she didn't want to be alone just yet. After a ten minute hike down the path they arrived at LaShaun's SUV. Chase climbed into the passenger side and gave her directions. His blue and gray Chevy truck was parked in another clearing not far away.

"I got one stop to make, and then we'll be on our way." Chase swung the passenger door open.

"This is turning into a big mystery, Deputy Broussard," LaShaun said.

"I've got to pick up a few supplies. Not sure I have everything I need at home," Chase replied.

LaShaun's felt a pleasant flutter when he shut the door firmly. She watched his lanky stride as he went to his truck, wondering if she'd lost her mind consorting with the law. Of course, she could simply drive home and ignore his invitation. Chase put the shotgun in the rack in the truck cab's back window. He turned, smiled, and waved to her. The pleasant flutter came back, and LaShaun turned the Mariner in his direction.

Chapter 7

They pulled up at the Black River Landing ten minutes later. Boaters milled around the parking lot. A few were preparing to launch boats. Others seemed to be coming in for the day. Cavalier's Country Store, constructed of weathered swamp cypress logs, sat to the left of the pier. The Cavalier family had been operating the store sixty years. Five or six people stood on a long wooden pier spaced out, taking their chances at catching a something tasty. Chase couldn't have chosen a more public place to be seen with her, outside of in the middle of town.

LaShaun pulled up beside his truck and let down the window when he walked over to her. "You sure this is a good idea?"

"Why wouldn't it be? I'll be back in a minute." Chase seemed so intent on his goal that he missed her meaning.

"If you say so," LaShaun mumbled as he left. Several people from Beau Chene looked at them and chattered away.

As he said, Chase came back with a plastic shopping bag. "Got what I need. Now I'm set."

"Uh-huh." LaShaun stared down several women who gawked at her.

Once again, she thought about turning around for home. At that moment Chase looked at her in his rear view mirror and waved, so she followed him again. Maybe he was the one with psychic powers. They drove down Highway 273, one of the small roads that crisscrossed Vermillion Parish. They were a good ten miles from the eastern boundary of her grandmother's land. They finally arrived at a gravel driveway that ended under a carport attached to a two-story house. The rest of the driveway curved off into a semi-circle in front of the house. Chase pulled onto it, and gestured for LaShaun to park under the carport.

"Don't want your car to get hot sitting out in the sun," he called. "Stay there and I'll be back after I put this in the kitchen."

"I can come in with you." LaShaun was talking to the air because Chase was gone. Seconds later he opened the front door and stood aside as she entered.

The parlor was a mixture of styles. Crocheted lace mats covered two tables. Two lovely antique lamps framed the sofa on end tables. She walked across a pretty rug of deep red, green and blue swirls lay on the floor. But masculine touches told her that he must live alone. Leather work boots sat in a corner next to the fireplace. An oak footstool with a lovely fabric cushioned top sat next to a chair, with a pair of socks draped across it. A wrench sat on the coffee table next to a stack of sports magazines.

"Nice, homey atmosphere," LaShaun said.

"Thanks. Have a seat." Chase disappeared down a hallway.

LaShaun took the liberty of following him to the kitchen. "You don't have to be so formal."

"My mama would be put out with me if I didn't entertain company right," he said over his shoulder.

"Your mama would be put out if she knew you had me in your house," LaShaun wisecracked. She took a few seconds to study several photos on the wall as she went down the hallway.

An arched doorway led into a wide kitchen with a panoramic view of the countryside. Cabinets of honey brown oak lined the walls. She guessed two doors in a corner opened into a refrigerator. The kitchen also featured a white cook top and a center island with copper pans. A matching oak breakfast table and chairs sat in an alcove to her left. Deep green granite covered the counters.

"Even doing the dishes must be a joy in here." LaShaun forgot to be suspicious or cautious as she went to the sink with a bay window, and the view that left her speechless. "You have my dream kitchen. Not that I cook."

Chase laughed. "I can't take credit. My sister and her husband had the old family house before me. They did the upgrades. You should see the master bedroom."

"S'cuse me?" LaShaun faced him and crossed her arms.

"I was just saying." Chase cleared his throat. "Kasey and Mike did a great job fixing up the place."

"Right." LaShaun pursed her lips.

"That wasn't a come on, honest. Not after what you've been through today." Chase wore a slight frown of concern.

LaShaun relaxed her stony expression. "I know. Being defensive is just a reflex action with me."

"I understand why." Chase grabbed a first aid kit from the kitchen counter. "Come over here and let me look at those."

LaShaun followed instructions. His large hands were gentle as he moistened a soft sterile cotton pad and cleaned the scratches on her arms with warm water. He moved with practiced care swabbing the cleaned skin with peroxide. When she hissed from the burning , he pursed his lips and blew lightly on her flesh. She gazed at the dark brown hair on his head so close. Without thinking, she lightly combed the fingers of her right hand through the waves. Chase looked into her eyes, and any barrier they might have been between them crumbled. LaShaun need to feel comforted and cared for after being on her own for so long. She kissed him hard. He didn't hesitate to respond, pressing her body to his strong chest. A very different and pleasurable burning sensation turned up the heat in her.

"Maybe we…" Chase mumbled between alternate kisses to her mouth and throat.

She cut off his sentence by covering his mouth with hers, then tugging at the belt around his waist. In seconds, they found themselves wrapped in a tight embrace. Hunger clouded LaShaun's awareness of her surroundings. When he touched her, she caressed him in turn. The heat between them felt like a separate living being. She could feel how much he wanted to be inside her, to know her completely. And she wanted him just as much. They ended up in the master bedroom, but LaShaun didn't notice the décor. Not for a long time. For only a few seconds LaShaun tensed. She'd been on her guard for so long that letting go took effort. Chase used his hands and tongue to convince her. She let him take control and pure bliss was her reward. When he was inside her, LaShaun lost all resistance. His moans mixed with hers until they both reached the height of ecstasy. After, they lay in each other's arms on top of the king-sized bed's comforter. LaShaun rested against his long, lean body. She finally looked around the bedroom through half-closed eyes.

"Nice room."

"Thanks," he murmured. "That was out of this world."

"Ah, you're making me blush." LaShaun poked his chest with a forefinger.

"Seriously, I had an out of body experience, like you turned into a whirlwind. Don't laugh but I heard music, like wind chimes. And I swear your eyes even changed color for a minute." Chase gave a long gasp of satisfaction. "Just... wow."

LaShaun sat up. "What else happened?"

"A lot of really, really good vibrations up and down my..." Chase reached for her, but LaShaun was off the bed. "Hey, come back here."

"In a minute."

She found her clothes in the hallway and took them back to the bedroom. To her relief the amulet was still in her shirt pocket. She draped her clothes on a chair and climbed next to him on the bed again. Chase opened his eyes, smiled, and pulled her down against his body. Chase rubbed her shoulder then touched the pendant between her breasts.

"You ever take this off?"

"It's my favorite piece of jewelry." She put the leather cord holding the amulet around his neck. LaShaun forced herself to speak in a light tone "I want you to wear yours all the time as well."

"Does this mean I'm your date for the prom?" Chase whispered.

LaShaun closed her eyes and pressed as close to him as she could. "Something like that."

* * *

One hour later LaShaun got home. Tasha was in the kitchen writing her notes in the folder for the nurse to review. After giving LaShaun a brief review of the day, the home health aide left. LaShaun went to Monmon Odette's bedroom.

"My, my, look at the time. You had a nice *long* ride in the country." Monmon Odette sat in the chair next to her bed. She peered at LaShaun over her reading glasses.

LaShaun smiled at her. "I missed the bayou more than I realized."

Monmon Odette put down the leather bound book she was reading. "Hmm, you been out communing with nature. No wonder you look so refreshed and relaxed."

LaShaun cleared her throat and changed the subject. "Being back home might not be all bad. Not that I'm looking forward to dealing with Rita. I didn't realize how much she resented me. And since when did she decide to take advice from Azalei is what I want to know."

Her grandmother's amused smile of mischief faded. She sighed and put the book on the nightstand. "I know. Something else I have to blame on myself. Promise me you won't play favorites with your children, Cher. All kind of evil is set in motion when you do."

"You did well by all your children and grandchildren," LaShaun protested.

"Non." Monmon Odette shook her head slowly. "Oh I tried to do for them all, but they knew. From the moment Francine was born. we had this connection different from my other children. I can't explain why I loved her so. That love did her no good."

"You chastise yourself too much, sweet grandmother." LaShaun pulled up the tapestry-covered footstool and sat near her.

"Ah well, there is no changing what was set in motion years ago." Monmon Odette wore a sad expression. She gestured that she wanted to get up and get into bed, and LaShaun helped her. Once tucked in she glanced at LaShaun. "Now what you gonna do about Rita?"

"I'll let the lawyers sort it out."

Monmon Odette merely nodded. She seemed weaker than usual. "Take care, child. Something wicked stirs."

Monmon Odette said so softly that LaShaun leaned down to hear her better. Instead of saying more, Monmon Odette pointed toward the window. LaShaun went to look, but only saw trees and shrubs. When she turned around to question Monmon Odette her eyes were closed. Moments later the soft raspy breathing signaled she had slipped into slumber.

Moments later LaShaun went to the back porch. She stood gazing across the backyard to the woods just beyond. Notes of her grandmother's favorite Creole tune carried on the early evening air that brushed LaShaun's cheek. Wind toyed with the leaves and long blades of palm shrubs. A sudden gust blew the scent of jasmine around her. LaShaun went down the back steps. A gentle force seemed to tug at her inside, moving her feet forward to what she called her "Magic Trees" as a child. In moments twilight shades of green and gray wrapped around her as she walked down a path. After a few yards, a gate seemed to spring right out of the lush foliage. An old wrought iron gate enclosed the

Rousselle family cemetery.

"Welcome home."

The sound whisked by LaShaun's right ear, a soft whisper. A swirl of leaves formed a circle; a smiling face. She closed her eyes and opened them again, wondering if she'd imagined it. . LaShaun stood staring down at the unmistakable shape until it shifted with another push of air. Mist crept along the ground.

"You've been waiting for me," LaShaun said.

"Yes," came the reply in a soft hiss.

Her heart thumped hard enough to cause pain in her chest. "Have you harmed anyone because of me?"

"For you."

A faint echo floated on the breeze; so slight the sound could have been an illusion. LaShaun felt disoriented as the leaves seemed to shift around her. Was she alone or surround by a crowd of others?

Then the air went still. Nothing moved, not even the small animals that filled every inch of Louisiana's verdant sub tropical landscape. Silence stretched until LaShaun thought she would scream. She steadied her breathing to calm down. A prickle started beneath LaShaun's skin. The sensation grew like fire ants on her arms and legs. Ignoring the trick meant to distract her, she began a prayer in Creole French, her voice low at first, then rising.

"Oh Holy St. Anthony, I pray to you the Saint of Miracles hear my prayer. Amen." LaShaun closed her eyes, swaying to the sound of chanting in her head. Then it stopped. Strengthened and resolute LaShaun opened her eyes again. "I want you gone."

The air crackled as though static electricity filled the atmosphere. The wind picked up. Leaves and branches swirled around LaShaun, dancing only inches from her body. Yet, none touched her. She tried to scream, but a vacuum sucked up the sound. Despite the riotous movement around her LaShaun heard nothing. Her scalp tingled, and she wanted to move, but her feet seemed rooted as though a magnet held her in place. Maybe it was her own fear at the wild force, and the knowledge that she had a hand in setting it loose. Then a clear male voice, accented with a strange musical lilt, answered her.

"I am yours, and you are mine."

* * *

The next day the home health aide arrived at her usual time in the morning. She came in and went into the bedroom. Moments later she called LaShaun to Monmon Odette's bedroom. Tasha's serious expression put LaShaun on alert.

"What's wrong?"

"Her pulse is a bit erratic and her blood pressure has dropped. I don't think all this drama is doing her any good." Tasha frowned at the numbers she written. "Good thing this is the day the nurse will come by."

LaShaun sat next to the bed. She kissed Monmon Odette's hand and watched her drift off to sleep. After a few moments, she gently placed her grandmother's hand on top of the quilt and patted it. She was tiptoeing toward the bedroom door when Monmon Odette's voice stopped her. LaShaun turned around. Her grandmother spoke with great effort.

"You saw, didn't you? Search the scrolls." Monmon Odette voice faded.

"What do you mean? I don't understand. Tell me, Monmon. Tell me where that spirit, that loa came from." LaShaun went to the bed and knelt next to it. "And how long has he inhabited our woods?"

Monmon Odette tried to speak again but let out a wheezing moan instead. A gurgling deep in her chest caused her to gasp, and her eyes grew cloudy. LaShaun grabbed her hand. The tips of her fingers had grown cold.

Tasha, come quick. Tasha!" LaShaun rubbed her grandmother's hands trying to push the creep of death from them. "No, no. Please give us more time."

Tasha rushed in with a male nurse right behind. "Let us take a look."

The nurse lifted Monmon Odette's eyelids then used the stethoscope around his neck to listen t her heart, then her breathing. He turned to Tasha. "Call 911."

Ten minutes felt like ten years to LaShaun. Ken explained in stark detail that Monmon Odette's blood pressure had risen very high then dropped. He and Tasha continued to monitor her pulse and heart rate. Finally, sirens whined close. LaShaun ran to the front door and let them in. The next two hours blurred from frantic activity to waiting in the uncomfortable hospital chairs. Eventually the doctor came out. Her expression said it all.

"We got her blood pressure stabilized, but..." Dr. Hu sat down next to LaShaun. "You need to call the rest of the family."

LaShaun could only nod. She cried in a way she hadn't since Francine had died.

The doctor stepped aside and let a nurse attempt to

console her. After a few moments, LaShaun dried her eyes and assured the nurse she would be okay. The nurse left as LaShaun dialed Uncle Leo's home number into her cell phone. Five minutes later Deputy Broussard walked into the lobby. LaShaun looked at him but kept on talking. Uncle Leo promised to assemble the rest of the family then hung up. LaShaun closed the flip phone. Chase sat down in one of the plastic and vinyl chairs in the row facing LaShaun.

"You must have the 911 call on your radio, right? I'm glad you're here." LaShaun took his hand.

"I'm not here about your grandmother." Chase shook his head. "But yeah, we knew you'd be here because of the 911 call."

"We?"

"This is a bad time to talk about this, but Azalei turned up and--"

"Good. Lock her up, and put Rita in the same cell while you're at it," LaShaun said. Then she breathed in and out to steady her nerves. "Look, I'm just upset right now. I can deal with those two later."

"We have to talk about this now, and it's not good," Chase said. He lightly brushed his fingers against LaShaun's left cheek, but dropped his hand at the sound of footsteps and stood.

"Hello, LaShaun." Sheriff Triche glanced at Chase, but said nothing.

Deputy Gautreau crossed his arms. "You don't have a call here. In fact you went off duty thirty minutes ago."

"Why are you here?" LaShaun snapped.

"To arrest you, *ma'am*." Deputy Gautreau wore a nasty grin. He unhooked metal handcuffs from the belt around his waist. "For kidnapping, assault, and suspicion of murder."

"Don't be ridiculous." LaShaun looked to Chase for answers.

Sheriff Triche spoke instead. "Azalei is back, LaShaun."

"Then question them because they're partners in crime. Just leave me alone so I can take care of my grandmother." LaShaun glared at them.

"We can't find Rita," Sheriff Triche replied.

"Azalei is bound to know where she is," LaShaun replied. She closed her eyes for a few seconds then opened them. "My grandmother is dying and you need me to do your jobs? Just ask Azalei."

"Azalei isn't talking, LaShaun," Chase said quietly.

"Of course not. She doesn't want to go to jail," LaShaun replied.

"She's not talking because she can't, and you know why. Let's not play these games, Sheriff. We know she did it." Gautreau moved toward LaShaun.

Chase planted a hand on his chest. "Not another step."

"Stop it you two," Sheriff Triche barked as the two deputies glared at each other. "We found Azalei in the woods on the eastern edge of your grandmama's property, LaShaun. In her mental state I doubt she'd talk even if she could."

"What do you mean she can't talk?" LaShaun turned to Chase.

"Because you had her tongue cut off," Gautreau answered before Chase could reply.

LaShaun gasped. The floor shifted beneath her feet. The walls seemed to sag in on her and she felt sick to her stomach. Swirling darkness closed over her as she slumped to the floor.

Chapter 8

A nurse practitioner examined LaShaun and observed her for thirty minutes before she allowed Sheriff Triche to question her. Stress and lack of food were the two causes of LaShaun's dizzy spell. Tasha agreed to sit with Monmon Odette until her shift ended. Monmon Odette had suffered a stroke, and she was still unconscious. Assured that her condition had not changed, LaShaun followed the sheriff to a small conference room the hospital administrator, under protest, made available. The stern older woman scowled at him and the two deputies. Deputy Gautreau wore a sour expression to make plain he wanted to take LaShaun to the station for booking. After being put in his place three times, he shut up when Sheriff Triche threatened to toss him out of the interview entirely. Chase remained silent through their exchange. Once they settled in the faux leather brown chairs arranged around an oval table, Sheriff Triche tapped a finger on the oak surface for a few seconds before he spoke.

"We don't have probable cause to charge you with felony assault on Azalei."

"Which could be attempted first degree murder because of how bad you beat her," Deputy Gautreau blurted out. He ignored the blistering look from his boss.

"Based on all the hoopla y'all been havin' you understand we got to question you," Sheriff Triche said.

"I know." LaShaun took a sip from the bottle of spring water one of the nurses gave her.

"Maybe we should wait, Sheriff. I'm not sure she's

up to this." Chase looked at LaShaun. Worry seemed to make his eyes even darker.

"I'm okay. Look, Azalei wasn't exactly my favorite cousin. Everybody knows that. But I want you to find out what happened to her, and find Rita. So I'm willing to help all I can." LaShaun fought off the chill not caused by the hospital vent above them.

"Very decent of you." Deputy Gautreau gave a grunt.

"Okay, that's it. Out." Sheriff Triche nodded toward the door to emphasize his point. Gautreau left without saying anything more. The sheriff turned back to LaShaun. "When was the last time you saw Azalei and Rita?"

"Three days ago at the family meeting. I went to Rita's house to talk to her, but she wouldn't answer the door. I didn't do anything to either of them." LaShaun breathed in and out to steady her raw nerves.

"Take your time," Chase said quietly.

"I was pissed at the way Rita and Azalei tried to take advantage of Monmon Odette. But Monmon's lawyer assured us that we had a good chance of tossing out that power of attorney."

"What?" Sheriff Triche leaned forward.

"Rita had Monmon Odette give her power of attorney. Then we found out that money had gone missing, a lot of money." LaShaun saw the sheriff's eyes widen slightly. "I was going through the court system to work things out. "

"Give me a time line on where you've been the past three days."

For almost two hours, Sheriff Triche went over every waking moment of every day in LaShaun's life for the previous seventy-two hour period. LaShaun felt shaken despite her calm exterior, but not because she seemed the likely suspect. Chase hovered nearby as though ready to catch her if she fell again. Sheriff Triche's disapproval showed on his face, but the older man said nothing to Chase. Finally, Sheriff Triche heaved a sigh.

"Alright, that's about it for now. I expect folks are going to think you attacked Azalei and did something to Rita. I just hope she's off hiding cause she's scared." The sheriff stood.

"I do, too." LaShaun rubbed her eyes.

"Maybe you better get some rest. You can't help your grandmother by falling out. Besides, she's got medical professionals steps away." Sheriff Triche's tone sounded less like the lawman.

"I want to be close by in case anything happens." LaShaun couldn't bring herself to say out loud that her grandmother might well die soon.

"I understand. Sorry for all your troubles." Sheriff Triche nodded. After one last long look at Chase, he left.

Chase went with LaShaun back to the critical care unit. Tasha and the nurse assured her that Monmon Odette was stable. Yet, the hospital atmosphere seemed to signal death. Long shadows along the hospital corridor created a gloomy atmosphere. The smell of disinfectant increased the effect.

"It's almost seven and getting dark out. You've been here for hours. I think you should go home, shower and sleep. Come back later tonight if it makes you feel better." Tasha put an arm around LaShaun.

Uncle Leo walked up as Tasha spoke. "Me and my

wife gonna be here awhile, LaShaun. She's right. Go on home."

"See? Mrs. Rousselle has an army of folks standing by for her," Tasha said with a smile.

"I'll be back by ten, Uncle Leo. You have my cell phone number if anything happens." LaShaun looked at them both.

"Stay and get some sleep. We'll call you the minute anything changes, I swear." Tasha gave her another pat on the shoulder then went back to look in on Monmon Odette. Uncle Leo followed her.

"Your grandmother would want you to take care of yourself," Chase said softly. "Come on, I'll drive. You look worn out."

Part of her wanted to object, but exhaustion gripped her. She walked beside him out of the hospital to the parking lot. LaShaun got into his truck. He slammed the passenger door shut, then got in and drove off. When LaShaun opened her eyes again Chase was gently tugging on her arm. He helped her climb down from on the running board of the truck. They were at his house.

"This isn't a smart idea for a lot of reasons. Your boss is already looking at you funny." LaShaun didn't resist as he grabbed her hand and led her to the front porch steps. She yawned.

"You shouldn't be alone after everything that's happened. Which of your relatives would you like to spend the night with?" Chase unlocked his door and clicked the remote of his security system.

LaShaun faced him once he'd closed the front door. "You've got a career and reputation to consider. Not to mention what your family will think."

"Let me worry about that." Chase locked the door and set the alarm. "Take a warm relaxing shower, and grab that LSU t-shirt in the top drawer of the dresser. That should fit you like a big sleep shirt. I'll brew some herbal tea to help us both sleep."

"Yes sir." LaShaun saluted.

When he grinned back at her, she felt a rush of pleasure. Chase headed toward the kitchen. "Take your time and let the water work its magic."

"I still say you should stay away from me," LaShaun called. When he didn't turn around, she shrugged and did as instructed.

He was right. Standing under the warm water coming from the rainfall showerhead caused much of the tension in her body to slip away. The master bathroom seemed designed to be a refuge. Soft tan marble surrounded the shower stall. A huge tub with several water jets could easily accommodate two people. Soft lighting and the smell of soap almost made the horrible events of the past few hours slip away. But not quite. LaShaun couldn't get Sheriff Triche's words out of her head. She slipped into the t-shirt and went to the vanity. Steam covered the wide oval mirror above the long counter. LaShaun bent over to rummage through a drawer, and finally found a comb and tortoise shell hairbrush. When she looked into the mirror again the outline of a grinning faced stared back at her. She froze for a few seconds then backed away. The comb and brush slipped from her fingers and clattered onto the tile floor.

"Tea's ready. Hey, you okay in there?" Chase said through the door.

"Uh, uh." LaShaun pressed her against the wall,

breathing in deep gulps of the humid air caused by her shower.

"LaShaun, honey, say something. Let me know you're okay."

When he twisted the door knob, LaShaun's head cleared. She whispered a hasty short prayer Monmon Odette had taught her as a child. Gathering inner strength, she continued to whisper as she angrily swiped at the image on the mirror. The soft tapping stopped. She took a few moments to steady herself.

"I'm, uh, I'm fine; just still a little tired. I'll be out in a minute."

When she opened the door Chase pulled her into his arms and kissed her forehead. "Of course you're not okay. You've been through hell."

Before she knew it LaShaun started to cry and shiver. After a few minutes, she pulled herself together. "I've got to stop this. I hate going all weepy like an idiot."

"You're entitled to be a weepy idiot," Chase said softly into her hair.

"Oh, gee thanks." LaShaun laughed and playfully slapped his shoulder . She pushed him away from the bathroom as she looked over her shoulder. "Where's that tea you promised? Or is making me feel all sentimental just a sneaky way to get me into a wet t-shirt?"

"Hmm, hadn't thought of that. But even dry you fill out that thing nicely." Chase grinned as he looked down at her. "To the kitchen, ma'am."

"I'm following your lead," LaShaun replied. "I better check to see if Tasha or the nurse called my cell."

"I checked already, and no, they haven't called."

Chase pointed to the two steaming mugs on a hot plate. "Your clothes are in the washer."

"You're going to spoil me if this keeps up." LaShaun breathed in the aroma coming from the cup then sipped.

"The way I see it you're due some TLC." Chase sat next to on a stool at the counter.

She put down the mug. "Thank you for being so thoughtful, and I know you mean well…"

"Yeah, I do." Chase took her hands in his.

"But."

"I could see it coming," Chase joked.

"Seriously, Chase. You want to run for sheriff, and you should. This parish could use someone like you. I don't want to be the reason your dream doesn't come true." LaShaun pulled away. "I really should drink this tea, wait for my clothes to dry and let you drive me home."

"That would seem sensible." Chase brushed her hair behind her right ear. "Except I'm not feeling sensible right now. I can't turn away when you need a friend."

"There's a little matter of my history, Deputy Broussard. Remember I was a suspect in a murder investigation. A lot of folks still believe I was in on it." LaShaun glanced at the bay window across from them. Was that a flash of something moving, or her imagination? She blinked and saw nothing. Chase's deep voice soothed her anxiety.

"That was a real whodunit with all kinds of suspects."

She tensed and stared at him. "What do you think?"

"The Sheriff and the DA got it right. Everything points to Kyle Singleton. He had motive, Trosclair was not only going to fire him, but he made it clear he was going to ruin his career. Singleton had means, and trace evidence in his SUV put Trosclair in it. I doubt he did it alone, but I don't think you were his accomplice."

"They could never prove Quentin was involved either, and Singleton wouldn't talk. He got an expensive attorney. I'm guessing Quentin's grandmother paid for that in exchange for his silence."

"Why would she help the man who killed her husband?" Chase frowned.

"They didn't have a happy marriage. The old man treated the poor woman like dirt, even in front of other people. He thought Quentin was a spoiled screw-up. My guess is she knew Quentin helped him, and she would do anything for her precious only grandson."

"Sounds like Kyle Singleton solved a nasty problem for them both," Chase murmured.

"I'd bet that Mrs. Trosclair and Quentin paid him handsomely to do his time and keep his mouth shut. He'll probably do his fifteen years and head for a nice, sunny beach somewhere with no money worries. "

"You don't' know?" Chase blinked at her in surprise.

"Know what, he's out on parole?"

"Yeah, you could say that. He left in a body bag. Another prisoner stabbed him to death two weeks before he was going before the parole board. I asked around. Seems the word was he had a good chance of getting out." Chase stared at her.

"Damn," LaShaun said and sat back in her chair.

"Bad luck?" Chase's dark eyebrows arched as he

gazed at LaShaun waiting for a reaction.

LaShaun felt a familiar tingle. Of course, Singleton's murder wasn't simply bad luck. The image of Quentin's confident swagger flashed into memory like a bad video re-wind. "His bad luck started when he crossed Claude Trosclair and thought he trust Quentin."

"Yeah. Singleton didn't have any incentive to protect you, He could have easily given you up as the murderer. So why didn't he?"

"He was terrified that I'd put a bad mojo on him?"

Chase grinned and shook his head. "For whatever reason, he didn't. The file shows the investigators couldn't connect you to the murder. Sheriff Triche personally checked your alibi, motive and if you had the means. I read the interview transcript. Sheriff Triche told the lead investigator back then not to waste his time. Singleton took a deal and avoided a trial."

"I see." LaShaun thought about that file. She would give just about anything to spend time reading every page.

"There are some loose ends, but with Singleton in prison nobody cared. Not Sheriff Triche and not the district attorney. Case closed." Chase continued to study LaShaun.

"You expect me to spill some secrets and fill in the blanks?" LaShaun said, and then yawned widely.

"I expect you to get some much needed sleep."

A musical tune made them both jump, then search for their cell phones. Chase grabbed his and held it up. LaShaun stood watching him as the tension in her muscles gripped her gain.

"It's me. Hello. Yes, sir, I'll be in at six in the morning. Good night." Chase ended the call. He looked at LaShaun. "They've found a woman's body. It's Rita."

LaShaun's heart beat so fast her chest hurt. She leaned against the breakfast bar gripping the marble edge. She asked the question though she already knew the answer. "Are they sure?"

Chase nodded then opened his arms. LaShaun shook her head slowly and covered her face with both hands. His strong arms and soothing voice got her through the night.

Chapter 9

The next three days went by fast. LaShaun got through the hours by putting one foot in front of the other. She felt trapped in a heavy fog of misery. Yet, she had to keep going for her grandmother. Decisions had to be made about her medical care, the financial mess Rita created, and how to manage the assets left. The lurid details of Azalei's injuries and Rita's murder brought a herd of reporters from as far away as Houston, Texas. The locals were only too happy to fill them in on rumors of voodoo. Claude Trosclair's murder became news again as well. By Thursday morning, LaShaun had to go through another round of questioning, this time at the Sheriff's station with the DA sitting in.

Savannah met her at the station. Within ten minutes, they were ushered into an interview room. Scott Hazelton, the new DA who had won election with his tough on crime stance, wore a suitably grim expression. Sheriff Triche's face had deep lines etched into it and dark circles under his eyes. His skin looked grayish. LaShaun wondered if he could make it through the next hour, much less another seven months until he retired. Deputy Gautreau stood to the right of the DA with a satisfied look stamped on his broad features. A young woman with shoulder length blonde hair in a dark gray suit sat next to the DA. Introduced as Brenda Crandall, she was Hazelton's assistant DA.

Sheriff Triche led the questioning and started with broad strokes, where had LaShaun been and with whom. He didn't ask about Rita or Azalei at first. Then the DA stepped in. He narrowed the focus to LaShaun's conflict with both victims. The assistant DA took over with more questions. After forty-five minutes, Savannah stopped writing and interrupted the interrogation.

"Okay, now you're asking the same questions in a different way. My client won't give different answers. So just let me sum this up and save us all time." Savannah consulted her notes on a yellow legal pad. "You have no physical evidence implicating my client. Nothing proves my client had the means to commit the assault or murder. You don't even know if the two women were together when they were attacked, or if we're talking about two different perpetrators, and Ms. Rousselle's motive is shaky."

"Circumstantial evidence sends a lot of people to prison," Deputy Gautreau replied. He ignored the way Sheriff Triche frowned at him.

"We're asking Ms. Rousselle questions so we can follow all leads. Your client did have heated confrontations more than once with both the victims. So it's only natural that we'd talk to her." The DA wore an impassive expression. "And we appreciate your client's willingness to cooperate."

"Good. So I'd say we're done here." Savannah zipped the leather portfolio that held her legal pad, picked up her purse, and stood. LaShaun followed her lead and also stood.

Deputy Gautreau stepped forward to block the exit. "Wait a damn minute, she ain't just walkin' outta here. She threatened both the victims about the old lady's money. Who else could have done it?"

"That would be your job to find out, deputy,"

Savannah shot back. "And you'd be doing it a whole lot better if you didn't jump to conclusions based on rumor and gossip. Goodbye, Sheriff. Mr. Hazleton. Let's go LaShaun."

In spite of Deputy Gautreau's menacing glare, Savannah went around him and opened the door to the interview room. She and LaShaun walked out. Sheriff Triche pulled one hand over his face and let out grunt. The DA and his assistant stood.

"We'll be in touch," Hazleton called out.

"Fine," Savannah replied over her shoulder as she kept walking. Once they were outside in the early spring sunshine Savannah let out a noisy breath. "Meet me at my office."

LaShaun, still shaken, nodded. She climbed in her SUV and made the short drive to downtown Beau Chene. She found a parking spot on the street about a half block from Savannah's office. Judging by the stares she got as she walked along the sidewalk the word was out. Savannah arrived in her car and went around to park behind the office. LaShaun went in first and Savannah came in minutes after. Savannah's paralegal was on the phone in the small lobby, the edge of frustration clear in his tone. He hung up and it rung again. Buttons on three the two extra lines were blinking.

"Reporters have been blowing up the phone all morning. How did they know y'all left the sheriff's station so fast?" Jarius, Savannah's young paralegal, shook his head.

"You kidding me? In this town I'd be surprised if they didn't have my shoe size by now." Savannah marched to her office. She dropped the portfolio on the desk and put her purse in a drawer. She was about to sit at down, but changed her mind. " Hey Jarius, lock the front door in case some of them come calling."

"You got it, boss," Jarius said. Seconds later he knocked then came in with two frosted mugs and bottles of root beer. He put the tray on the edge of Savannah's desk and left just as quickly.

LaShaun sat down in one of the leather chairs. "This is bad."

"If you mean the case against you is bad, you're right." Savannah poured the root beer from the bottles into the two mugs. She picked up one, drank and sighed then sat at her desk. "Now you know another reason I hired that young man. He knows what a boss wants, and when she wants it."

For the first time LaShaun smiled, but it didn't last. She grabbed the mug. "Nice to have somebody you can count on."

Savannah looked at her for few moments. "How are you holding up?"

"Other than being a police suspect in two major crimes? Life is good." LaShaun lost her taste for the root beer.

"Not to mention worrying about your grandmother," Savannah said.

"I don't care about being questioned because I didn't do anything. Not that I didn't get mad enough to give them both a good butt kicking."

"Let's keep that kind of talk within these four walls." Savannah pointed at her.

"Okay, okay." LaShaun took a deep breath. "What I mean is we had our differences, but doing something so monstrous would never enter my mind."

"Good, good. That's a perfect quotable statement." Savannah nodded, and put down her mug to scribble notes.

"It happens to be true. Or does my lawyer think I did it?"

Savannah stopped writing. "No, I don't. You've changed. If I didn't think that I would have referred you to another lawyer."

"That makes two of us in the entire state that believes I'm innocent." LaShaun massaged the tightness in her neck with both hands.

"Three. Deputy Broussard is in your corner." Savannah wore a slight frown and tapped one foot.

"I hear the silent 'but' hanging from that statement."

"It could complicate matters. Especially for him, but I'm sure he knows that. Of course, it could be a good thing. He's well liked around here. From what I hear, most of his support comes from younger people, and the growing retiree population that has moved from outside the parish. In fact a lot of them are from other states." Savannah rocked her chair back and forth. "I don't know. Maybe his belief in you could be a plus."

"Or they could question his judgment, maybe even his integrity." LaShaun got up and stared out of the window at the quaint downtown so carefully created by the chamber of commerce, and other town leaders. "Do they want a sheriff whose lover is voodoo priestess and two time murder suspect?"

The lawyer's eyebrows shot up. "So things have progressed that far. Yeah, that's could be a definite problem."

"You think?" LaShaun retorted with a sharp laugh.

"The word 'problem' doesn't begin to cover it."

Savannah cleared her throat. "Maybe y'all should take a break until things cool down and we find out what really happened."

"I've told him that." LaShaun felt a hollow sensation at the thought. "

"And of course being a sensible lawman he agrees?"

LaShaun faced Savannah. "No, and it scares me more than just about anything else. I don't want to ruin any more lives than I already have."

"You pulled some tricks in your day, but that's a little dramatic." Savannah raised a hand. "Let me finish. I'll admit that for a long time I believed that maybe you killed Claude Trosclair, but then that didn't add up. So I thought maybe you'd put Quentin up to it. But, let's be real, Quentin hated his grandfather. He wanted the family fortune, so he didn't need any encouragement."

"But I may have set events in motion." LaShaun swallowed hard. "And now I'm back and this happens."

"You're taking on too much guilt." Savannah shook her head.

"Sometimes the evil we set loose just keeps on causing destruction. I don't want to be the cause of anymore casualties, especially not Chase." LaShaun squeezed her eyes shut, but not tight enough to stop the tears.

"Then stop it."

LaShaun opened her eyes, and Savannah was standing in front of her with a wad of tissues in one hand. She gazed at Savannah in silence for a few moments then took the tissue, and wiped her eyes. "What did you just say?"

"I'm guessing either you know a way to fight back, or can figure it out," Savannah said. Gone was the educated, modern woman. Savannah had grown up in the bayou country like LaShaun. Like other natives, she didn't dismiss the folk tales and ways of the past as superstitious nonsense. Though outsiders found it strange, people of the swamps saw no conflict between conventional religion and the old beliefs in the spirit world. In fact, both traditions agreed, the battle between good and evil was real, and constant.

LaShaun breathed in and out to steel herself. "Yes. I've got to find a way."

* * *

Monmon Odette still lay in the critical care unit of Vermilion Hospital on the day of Rita's funeral. The stroke left her in weak on the right side of her body, and unable to speak clearly. Though they hadn't told her about Azalei and Rita, LaShaun sensed she knew something terrible had happened. Uncle Leo and Uncle Albert shocked LaShaun by being supportive. Then the logic behind their behavior became clear. LaShaun controlled Monmon Odette's considerable estate. Her seemingly supportive uncles had their own interests in mind.

LaShaun came out of the critical care unit. She dressed in a simple black skirt and blouse for the funeral. Both uncles were in the hallway wearing dark suits talking low to each other. Except for their differences in height, they looked alike. They wore twin solemn expressions as well. Uncle Leo saw LaShaun first. He nodded in her direction, and touched his brother on the shoulder. Uncle Albert stopped talking and they walked toward her.

"You sure going to the funeral is a good idea, Cher?" Uncle Leo's tone was soothing. "Some raw feelings about all this mess with the family, you know."

"Yeah, La-La," Uncle Albert put in, using LaShaun's childhood nickname that no one had called her in years.

"I'm not going to hide out like I did something wrong." LaShaun looked at them both. "Rita might have done some things that I didn't like, but she was family. I'm going to pay my respects."

"Then good thing we stopped by. We'll go with you. Leave your vehicle here. I'll drive us in my truck." Uncle Leo nodded as though that settled the question.

"Thanks."

LaShaun allowed him to hook his large hand under her elbow and lead the way. They all got into Uncle Leo's his fancy dark green special edition Ford F10 truck with an extended cab. In spite of her cynicism about their solicitous behavior, LaShaun was still grateful for their presence. They arrived at St. Augustine Catholic Church. Most of the mourners had already entered so they attracted little attention at first. Uncle Albert led them to a seat at the end of the middle row of pews, the section reserved for the family. A distant middle-aged cousin, Esmee sat on the other end with her adult daughter. When she noticed LaShaun between Uncle Leo and Uncle Albert her eyes widened, and she whispered to her daughter. Within seconds, the news passed up the family section. Heads swiveled back, and the murmuring continued until the priest spoke.   Rita's mother, Aunt Shirl, softly wept throughout the short mass. She leaned against Rita's stepfather. Rita's two half-sisters took turns sitting next to their mother to console her.

The small church resonated with the solemn notes from an organ as the service ended. Pallbearers rolled the casket out to the waiting hearse. Most of the mourners walked the short distance to the nearby church cemetery. Thirty minutes later. it was over. Rita was in the ground, and LaShaun was no closer to seeing the truth. She'd hoped that some message might come through, especially in the graveyard, but nothing. No chills along her spine, no prickle up her arms or strange shimmers in the air.

In spite of Uncle Leo and Uncle Albert protesting she was pushing her luck, LaShaun insisted they attend the repast. Family and friends had prepared a wonderful buffet of foods. The family was served first, and then the other mourners helped themselves. Rita's mother waved away a plate of food one of her daughters tried to give her. Then she spotted LaShaun. Conversation died away like a ripple through the crowd. When Aunt Shirl stood, her daughters and husband argued with her. Finally, she cut all three off.

"I said no. Now hush." Aunt Shirl brushed her youngest daughter's hand away. "Go on now, Chelette." Then she walked over to LaShaun.

"Maybe we better leave," Uncle Albert mumbled low to Uncle Leo.

"Let me talk to her first." Uncle Leo wore a smile as he walked to meet Aunt Shirl.

"Leo, thank you for comin'," Aunt Shirl said, but went past him to LaShaun. "You and me need to talk. We'll go in one of these rooms."

"I know you're upset, Shirl. But don't believe all kinds of wild talk going around." Uncle Albert motioned to Uncle Leo, who still stood in the middle of the hall looking stunned.

"I'm talkin' to LaShaun in private. Just stay out of this."

Aunt Shirl stared at them until they both took a step back. Then she jerked a thumb at LaShaun before going into the office. LaShaun followed her, closed the door, and steeled herself for an attack. Instead, Aunt Shirl sank onto a small sofa and closed her eyes.

"Before you say anything, Aunt Shirl, let me just say I would never have hurt Rita, not that way. We got into a fight sure, but I didn't... I couldn't." LaShaun stopped when Aunt Shirl looked up.

"Rita had it hard. I realize that now," Aunt Shirl said; her voice hoarse with emotion. "Her daddy and your mama looked so much alike, with that wild kind of good looks that made folks stare at 'em. Robert Rousselle had me with just one little old smile."

LaShaun sat down on one of the folding chairs in the room. "I don't really remember Uncle Robert. He wasn't around much when I was a kid."

"Humph, that says it all. Robert wasn't around much for anybody. He was too busy gambling, drinking, and going from club to club. But he could sing and play that guitar." Aunt Shirl sighed. "Rita didn't know him much better than you. Then I married, had more kids. She always felt like the red-headed stepchild as the old saying goes."

"And that Monmon Odette favored me," LaShaun said.

"Well she did. I'm not faulting you for that, but

118

your grandmother should have known better." Aunt Shirl looked at LaShaun. "But I gotta ask you plain, did you cause this horrible thing to happen to my child?"

"I swear before God, Aunt Shirl, I didn't have anything to do with Rita's death. LaShaun leaned forward. "*Nothing.*"

Aunt Shirl gazed at her in silence for a long time. Someone knocked on the door and she called out, "We're fine, just leave us for a minute."

"I want to find out who did this more than anyone, except you." LaShaun saw the pain in Aunt Shirl's eyes turned to a flash of anger.

"I want the scum to get the death penalty, and I want him to suffer first." Aunt Shirl clenched and unclenched her hands several times. Then she sank back against the sofa. "That won't bring my child back, but at least I'll get some justice."

"Do you believe me?" LaShaun said quietly.

Aunt Shirl blinked back from her grief and looked at LaShaun. "Folks will think I'm crazy, or that you put a mojo on me, but I do believe you. Then again, I never cared what folks thought anyway. Listen, Rita had some regrets. She was sorry for throwing in with Azalei and her crowd. She told me so. Seems like Rita didn't know just how deep the water was until she up to her neck. You know Azalei was running with that Quentin Trosclair."

"No," LaShaun replied. She decided not to mention Quentin's tantalizing hint at some connection between them.

"He's got more trouble than he's got money in the bank, and we know he's got a lot of that." Aunt Shirl grimaced. "Anyway, Rita said she thought she was having fun at first, but then something happened that made her see her new friends differently."

"What?" LaShaun felt a prickle along her arms.

Aunt Shirl shook her head slowly. "She wouldn't go into it, just said she needed to get away from them. From the look on her face, I figured it was bad, but I didn't push her. Now I wish I had."

"Did she mention anybody else? That could give the police a clue about who might have attacked them."

"She didn't say any other names, but they partied with some others, I do know that much. Look, I told the sheriff that Rita was partying hard, that maybe she dabbled in drugs. The blood tests showed she'd been smoking marijuana and had some other drugs in her system. Now she might have smoked weed, but I don't believe Rita would use meth or ecstasy. I want her name cleared, LaShaun."

"Yes, ma'am." LaShaun nodded. "But why not tell all this to the sheriff?"

"Sheriff Triche is sick. Didn't you hear? Something about his heart."

"Too bad." LaShaun remembered how pale and shaky Sheriff Triche looked a few days ago during her interview. "He's a good man."

"Yeah, more fair than any of those previous sheriffs." Aunt Shirl shrugged. "Time marches on. Anyway, the deputy that's itching to get the sheriff's job talked to us. I don't like him, or trust him either."

"Deputy Broussard is a good guy, Aunt Shirl."

"I'm talking about that Gautreau fella. There's talk that he was partying with Quentin and Azalei, but folks are too scared to do more than whisper that real low; and only to people they trust real good. Quentin and

Gautreau both got a reputation for being mean as a bucket of snakes." Aunt Shirl shook her head slowly. "Something ain't right. I figure you have a strong reason to find the truth. You don't want to end up in prison for something you didn't do."

LaShaun stood. "You're right about that. I don't know if I can, but I'm going to try to find out what really happened no matter who goes down."

Aunt Shirl looked up at her for a few moments then rose slowly from the sofa. Her face had lines of grief and exhaustion. She seemed to have run out of energy. "I know you have the gift, like your Monmon. Folks say one day it's gonna burn you up."

"Maybe." LaShaun knew she had to do more than look for facts in the human world. She thought back to the whispers in the woods, and the face that appeared to her.

"I know Rita felt bad about the way she dealt with Miz Odette. She had some jealousy toward you, that's the truth. But there was a time back when y'all were kids that Rita looked up to you. Forgive her, find her killer."

"I'll use whatever gift Le Bon Dieu gave me to find her killer," LaShaun promised.

Rita's mother gazed at LaShaun for a few minutes. "I never thought you was evil like a lotta folks said. Just headstrong like your Monmon and wild like your mama. We all make mistakes."

"Thanks, Aunt Shirl."

"But something bad always seems to follow your footsteps, LaShaun. I want you to stay away from my daughters. Just stay away."

Aunt Shirl took a step back, and circled around

LaShaun as though careful not to get too close. She went out of the room leaving LaShaun alone. Seconds later Uncle Leo came in. He looked around the room as if something in it would give him a clue about their conversation.

"You alright?" he said.

"Yes. I'm ready to leave." LaShaun walked out past him, and left the church annex building. People stared at her until she got into her uncle's truck.

Uncle Albert tried to begin conversation, but LaShaun's one-word answers soon discouraged him. She was glad when they arrived back at the hospital parking lot. She thanked them, then quickly left the truck and went into the hospital. Assured that there was no change in Monmon Odette's condition, LaShaun went home. She tried to take a nap, but the conversation with Aunt Shirl kept playing in her mind.

* * *

At ten o'clock the next morning LaShaun went back to the hospital. The doctors upgraded Monmon Odette's status from critical to serious. They moved her into a room. LaShaun continued to pay the home health agency to provide sitters in the hospital. After she got an update from nurse on duty, LaShaun entered the room. The nurse's assistant smiled at her as she came in.

"I'm just putting some lotion on her legs and arms. Tasha will be here about one o'clock." The petite woman continued to massage Monmon Odette's arms while she worked.

"Thank you. Y'all are taking real good care of

her." LaShaun appreciated the neatness of the bedding and the room in general.

"Thank you, ma'am. There now. I'm going to leave some notes with the nurse at the desk, and be on my way."

"Will the nurse need to come in any time soon?" LaShaun asked.

"No, ma'am. She just took her vitals. She won't to do that for another two hours. The IV meds and fluids are all set." She gave LaShaun a maternal pat on the arm as she left.

LaShaun waited until the door whisked shut quietly. She took an antique book from the leather tote she'd brought with her. Before opening it, LaShaun went to the door and looked out. The nurse's assistant spoke quietly to the nurses on duty. No one else was in the hallway. Reassured they would not be disturbed, LaShaun sat in the chair close to the hospital bed. The brown paper rustled softly as she smoothed out its fragile pages yellowed with age. The window blinds were half closed, and only a soft white light glowed in the room. Soon LaShaun was absorbed in reading the fancy script before her. She struggled to translate the Louisiana Creole French, a dying language rarely spoken even by the descendants of Creoles of color. Some words were unfamiliar. Still LaShaun understood enough to translate spellbinding Rousselle family secrets kept for a century or more.

"So you found it."

The raspy voice hardly sounded familiar. LaShaun started and looked around the room half expecting to see a phantom. Instead, her grandmother lay watching her, breathing heavily as though just a few words had been a huge effort. She grimaced and pursed her lips. LaShaun put the book aside quickly, and found a plastic pitcher of ice water. She poured some into a cup with a straw and helped her grandmother drink. Monmon Odette turned away to signal she'd had enough.

"I love you, granmér." LaShaun felt the need to say that before anything else because her grandmother was slipping away.

Monmon Odette moved her head slightly. "I love you as well, child. You've found the answer." Her words slurred and faded.

"Not yet, but I'm still looking." LaShaun put the cup down and leaned against the bed. She held Monmon Odette's hand.

"Not a question."

LaShaun studied her grandmother's expression for a long time. She read a message in those dark eyes that so many had tried to understand for decades. "You weren't asking me a question. You meant that I've already found the answer. It's in the book? But I don't understand. There are riddles and references."

"You must be…" Monmon Odette's word was jumbled. She breathed in and out then closed her eyes for a few seconds. Then she opened them to look at LaShaun. "Whole."

"What does that mean, Monmon? Monmon?"

LaShaun leaned in close to her grandmother's face. She smoothed the wrinkled brow gently with her hands. Monmon Odette's breathing became regular. Her eyes closed and she drifted off again.

"I shouldn't be questioning you anyway. This is my task, not your burden. I set this in motion." LaShaun sighed, kissed her grandmother's cheek, and sat down again.

"No, you did not." Her grandmother looked at LaShaun with clear eyes, and spoke in a strong voice. "I passed on to you a great evil, started by your ancestor Jacques Pierre. In my willful youth I carried on the ways of old and tempted fate."

LaShaun sprang up to stand near the bed again. She smiled. "Now don't talk nonsense. Once you get better we'll talk all about the ancestors and our family history."

"Forgive me, ma Cher, for the burden I leave."

Monmon Odette's voice died to a faint whisper. Her eyes became glazed over with an odd bluish cloudy appearance. She seemed to be looking through LaShaun at something else as lips quivered. LaShaun felt like ice had been poured over her head as chill bumps covered her arms. She gently took Monmon Odette's hand it, but it was stiff and unresponsive. Alerted by the change in the electronic monitoring unit, the nurse pushed through the door and went straight to Monmon Odette. Soon another nurse joined her.

"Stand back please."

LaShaun, feeling numb, nodded. She watched as they lifted her grandmother's eyelids and put a stethoscope to her chest. Moments later a young doctor came in. He took over, quietly speaking to the nurses.

"Would you wait outside, ma'am?"

"Yes," LaShaun replied.

She went to the hallway and whispered prayers for her dead grandmother's soul to be at peace. Ten minutes passed before the doctor came out to tell LaShaun what she already knew.

LYNN EMERY

Chapter 10

For the next two, days LaShaun went about the business of death. A parade of relatives came to the house, her uncles, numerous cousins, and two of Monmon Odette's surviving siblings. At Rhodes Funeral home the owner expressed his condolences repeatedly as they made the arrangements. LaShaun resisted his poorly disguised attempts to glean the inside story of her family and the recent events.

Once home, LaShaun went to the beautiful antique armoire in Monmon Odette's bedroom. In a secret drawer, she found her grandmother's wishes, written in Monmon Odette's fluid handwriting. Her grandmother had planned her services twenty years before. LaShaun could almost hear her voice saying, "I don't want my silly children making up the order of services. No tellin' what kind of nonsense they'll put down."

She spent another two hours simply looking through her grandmother's clothes, jewelry, and cosmetics. The scent of lavender sachet pillows tucked into drawers soothed LaShaun's aching heart.

Turning her attention to the old diaries brought on another sensation. A chill brushed across her arms as she settled into the stuffed chair to read. Fluid lines of handwriting transported her to the past once more. LaShaun read with fascination how her ancestors had schemed and used their gifts to survive in a harsh landscape of slavery and discrimination. Using the supernatural to gain wealth and power was a consistent thread. Included in the thick book were mundane descriptions of domestic life in the eighteenth and

LYNN EMERY

nineteenth centuries. Yet mixed in with the list of
household items and family recipes were spells. These
were the unique combination of the spiritual beliefs
from Africa and the Christian religion of the new world.
Once again, LaShaun read the passage that had
intrigued her; the one Monmon Odette seemed to speak
about even as she died.

Lucinda Gravois, Monmon Odette's great
grandmother, spoke of awaking a spirit that had its own
mind. This spirit had brought her wealth and helped her
family, but at a price. His hold grew until, with the help
of two women also skilled in the old religion, Lucinda
freed herself. She then talked about giving up the ways
of wickedness, and returning to the Catholic Church.
Obviously, her daughter had not agreed. Subsequent
generations, female especially, had used their gifts
again while still attending mass as faithful Catholics.

LaShaun learned the history of her family culture,
and the history of Creoles of Color in Vermillion
Parish. Even more, she sensed that the answer lay in the
pages. Yet the complete picture seemed just out of
reach. The room grew dark so she turned on the lamp in
the bedroom and kept reading. Totally immersed in the
story of her great great-uncle's fight to buy land in
1874, an insistent tapping sound startled her. It was
then that she realized the rest of the house was dark.
LaShaun felt a prickle along her spine at being alone.
She'd never been truly alone in her grandmother's
house. Thankfully, the large light outside had come on
at dusk. In minutes, she hurried around turning on lights
in the kitchen and living room. The tapping seemed to
follow her. Once she checked that the doors were
locked, LaShaun went back to the diaries.

LaShaun flipped back to the pages written so long ago. She repeated the prayer written over one hundred thirty years before her birth. The tapping stopped. She let out a long breath of relief too soon. A loud knock made her jump to her feet.

"LaShaun, It's me. Are you okay?"

"Yes, hold on."

She followed the sound to the kitchen door. His caring radiated through wall between them. LaShaun allowed herself the luxury of being happy to see him, even though she knew he shouldn't have come.

Chase peered through the window set in the door. His frown of worry was visible through the pale yellow curtain covering it. When LaShaun undid the locks and opened the door, he glanced around inside.

"Sure you're okay? I've been calling your grandmother's phone for over an hour. Then I tried your cell phone."

"Sorry to worry you. I turned the ringer volume down low on the phones so it wouldn't disturb Monmon when she was resting. And with reporters calling I didn't bother to turn them on again." LaShaun sighed.

"I know this is tough on you." Chase put his arms around her.

She let him hold her for a few minutes, but then stepped away. "I'm fine, really. So that was you tapping for five or ten minutes."

"I just got here and knocked a few times on the kitchen door. You think somebody is outside?" Chase went back to the door and peered out.

LaShaun followed and pulled him away from the window facing the woods. "No, this old house makes lots of noise every time the wind blows. Hey, you coming here is a seriously bad idea. I'm a suspect."

"And I'm here to question you," Chase said with a straight face.

"Yeah right. I'm sure the town councilmen would believe that. How is Sheriff Triche?" LaShaun moved farther away from him. She wanted to avoid the temptation to lean against his strong chest again.

"Not good. I hear he's going on medical leave until his official retirement date in September." Chase sat on a stool at the breakfast bar.

"And who's in charge until then?" LaShaun started a pot of coffee for them both without asking.

"If Brad's lobbying works he'll be chosen, He's got some local good old boys trying to influence the council. They're having a special meeting Friday morning."

"So in two days the man who wants to send me to prison could be in charge of enforcing the law. Great." LaShaun gave a short laugh empty of humor.

"They could choose me you know." Chase smiled at her.

"Which is why you need to stay far away from me. You've got common sense, so use it." LaShaun faced him.

"LaShaun--"

She held up a hand. "Even those progressive newcomers will start to wonder about you. Look at the facts. I was a suspect in a high profile murder when I was barely out of my teens. Now I'm accused of cutting off one cousin's tongue, leaving her for dead, and killing another cousin."

"Can I say something now, please?" Chase crossed

his arms.

LaShaun cleared her throat. "Go ahead."

"I happen to agree with you, but not the way you think," he said. "I care about finding out the truth and not compromising any investigation, especially this one. Even the appearance of impropriety could not only short circuit catching a killer, but put you in danger."

"So we agree that you should stay away, that we shouldn't see each other again. Great." LaShaun tried to smile, but her face wouldn't cooperate. Instead she covered she started to cry.

"Hey, hey, don't you worry." Chase crossed to her in seconds and pulled her hands away. He kissed her with loving tenderness. "As long as I'm on the earth you'll never be alone."

LaShaun held him close for a few moments then pulled herself together again. "You've got to be super careful. Gautreau will be watching every move you make. I wouldn't be surprised if he as you followed."

"On these lonely country roads I'd spot a tail in a New York second." Chase rocked her gently as he spoke. Then he buried his face in the thick curls of her hair. "You smell like heaven."

"Some folks will think you're consorting with one of the devil's daughters," she said, her words muffled against his chest.

"What a load of bull." Chase laughed.

She thought about the loa. LaShaun opened the top button of his cotton shirt and touched the pendant she'd given him on a chain around his neck. She sighed with relief then looked up at him. With the tip of one finger, she traced the line of his strong jaw. When his lips parted slightly, LaShaun gave in to temptation and kissed him.

"Thanks for making me feel better than I have in the past seven days." LaShaun shook free of his reassuring embrace. Starting now she would have to get used to being without him. "With everything going on I haven't had a chance to ask about Azalei."

Chase's expression turned grim. "She was beaten up pretty bad. But the doctors say with rehab she could talk again, even with part of her tongue gone. The question is will she recover mentally. She retreated into a world of her own. Her mother is making all kinds of wild accusations about you."

"Let me guess; she says I called on my demon minions to attack Azalei and Rita."

"Pretty much. She says you dance with evil spirits at midnight. She said woods behind this house and the family cemetery are haunted." Chase shook his head. "I wish I could joke about that stuff, but under the circumstances."

"A lot of people around here believe in the gris-gris and mojos." LaShaun thought about the diaries only a few feet away in her grandmother's bedroom. "It's funny."

"I'm not laughing," Chase said in a dry tone.

"What goes around comes around. My family has succeeded only too well convincing people that we do have supernatural powers." LaShaun shrugged.

"Yeah, well they should have sense enough to know better." Chase went to the cabinet and got out two of her grandmother's everyday coffee cups.

He continued to talk, but his voice faded away. LaShaun thought she could hear her grandmother's soft chuckle. She suddenly had a light-headed sensation, and Chase seemed far away instead of only a few feet from her. Soft bumping drew LaShaun's attention to the window. A large white moth hit the glass twice before lighting on it, its wings fluttering.

"Family legends and ghost stories are fun told around a fire on a cold night. We have a few tall tales in the Broussard family. But let's be honest, most of that stuff had a down to earth, very commonsense explanation. Here's your coffee, sweetie." Chase extended the cup to her.

LaShaun blinked as the strange sensation passed, and the room came back into sharp focus. The white moth and laughter vanished at the same time. Or maybe she had imagined both. "Down to earth," she murmured.

"Hey," Chase waved a hand in front of her face. He put the cup down on the counter. "I think you're putting on a brave face for me. I'll stay the night. On the sofa out of respect for your grandmother's memory," he added in a prim tone.

"You don't have to do that. Monmon Odette was anything but conventional, and I think she liked the idea of you and me together." LaShaun thought back to her grandmother's smile when she saw them together, and her talk of children. Then LaShaun said low, "Now that is nonsense."

"Did you say something?" Chase looked down at her.

"No. I should make you go." LaShaun breathed in the scent of his skin.

"We can avoid each other a little later," Chase said.

They went to LaShaun's bedroom and undressed. Once in bed, they simply wrapped around each other.

They whispered softly about their respective childhood memories, life in Vermillion Parish and ordinary family traditions; everything else but murder, magic and the dreadful possibilities that waited just outside in the dark.

* * *

In the space of less than two weeks, St. Augustine Church was the site of another high profile funeral. Two deputies stood outside in the sunshine near their motorcycles, ready to lead the funeral procession. Inside every pew was full. The church musician played soft music on the organ. LaShaun stood in a corner with Father Metoyer observing the crowd. She was aware of every movement and murmur rippling around her. The sound of clicking made Father Metoyer glared at a news photographer.

"Excuse me, child."

Father Metoyer disappeared through a door behind the altar. Moments later two strapping adolescent boys dressed in cassocks over dark suits politely, yet firmly escorted the photographer outside. Reporters remained in seats near the church entrance, trying to be invisible so they could get every detail. Monmon Odette no doubt would have laughed long and hard at the show. LaShaun sat down on the front pew of the family section next to her Uncle Albert and Uncle Leo. Moments later a rising tide of whispers caused all three of them to turn around. Aunt Leah made a dramatic entrance with Azalei supported between her and her husband. Aunt Leah wore dress made of delicate lace black. Azalei wore a dark gray skirt and matching jacket. She seemed dazed and unaware of her surroundings. They made their way up the center aisle. Father Metoyer met them halfway. After a muted exchange, he led the trio to far end of the first pew away from LaShaun. Aunt Leah gave her brothers a look that could have melted steel, but said nothing.

"Can't believe she brought Azalei out here in that condition. Going to a funeral could push her over the edge," Uncle Albert whispered to Uncle Leo.

"Look at her, Al. That girl's over the edge and at the bottom already."

Uncle Albert nodded slowly. The host of relatives on the rows behind them exchanged similar thoughts. LaShaun ignored the background noise and focused on Azalei. Her cousin had scratches on one side of her face, but they did not look deep. One arm was in a sling. Yet, her vacant expression chilled LaShaun the most. The serious damage seemed to be to her mind instead of her body. When Aunt Leah noticed LaShaun staring at them, she pulled Azalei closer to her protectively. The gesture caused more murmuring until Father Metoyer spoke.

"Peace be unto you all," he boomed.

His strong voice and formidable gaze clearly communicated that meant they should shut up. A hush followed his words. Satisfied he'd gotten his message across the priest proceeded with the funeral mass.

Monmon Odette lay in the open white coffin with shiny brass hardware. LaShaun gazed ahead at her grandmother with dry eyes. She had shed her tears in private. For now, she was calm, conscious of the curious gazes from the others. Old lessons from her grandmother lingered. Monmon Odette had always said, "If you show emotion before your enemies let it be for a purpose. When it's time to show folks you're not to be played with, let them see your wrath. When you need to soften someone to your will, let them see you cry. Control is the key to power."

LaShaun had no need to prove to others that she felt a loss. Rita's mother came into the church through a side door. When she walked toward LaShaun the crowd seemed to take in another collective deep breath. Aunt Shirl ignored them. Her husband walked beside her, a protective arm around her waist. LaShaun motioned to a male cousin who made sure they found a place in the family section.

LaShaun went through the motions of the Funeral Rites, reciting the prayers on autopilot. Her grandmother lived on in many ways, her spirit too strong to simply wisp away. And somehow, LaShaun didn't believe Monmon Odette was through with her family. She loved being in control too much to simply float into the next life; not with so much left undone in this one. Monmon Odette had said as much before she closed her eyes for the final time.

"Cher, it's time we leave for the cemetery," Father Metoyer said quietly.

LaShaun blinked out of her reverie. "Yes, Father."

Father Metoyer took LaShaun's hand and led her out ahead of the others behind the casket. Outside the church LaShaun blinked in the bright sunshine. She put on sunglasses then got into the white limo. There was a brief commotion as Aunt Leah loudly announced she would not ride in the limo as "that she-devil." A funeral home employee quickly led her away to the second of four family cars LaShaun had arranged. Uncle Leo helped Monmon Odette's eighty-nine year old elder sister, Emerald, get settled onto the seat of the limo. Uncle Albert assisted Great Aunt Geraldine, a sprightly seventy-seven year old. He slipped in and sat next to LaShaun. Great Aunt Emerald studied LaShaun for a few moments.

"May my sister rest in peace at last." Great Aunt Emerald looked away. Then she and Aunt Geraldine spoke quietly in Creole French.

Two motorcycle deputies revved their motors ready to lead the procession to the Rousselle Family Cemetery seven miles away. Uncle Albert's wife came to the window and looked at her husband a few second then climbed into the vehicle. Uncle Theo's wife dared to sit on the seat next to LaShaun. She gave LaShaun a nervous smile then looked away. Uncle Theo stood just at the door still talking to people, accepting handshakes and condolences.

"Come on, Theo. You're holding everybody up," Uncle Albert grumbled to his brother.

"Right, right," Uncle Theo replied. Still he took another few moments to slap a few backs before he got in.

"I see we got two extra escorts from the sheriff's department," Uncle Albert said. He frowned. "That's gonna cost us a fortune."

His wife tapped his knee. "Shush, LaShaun wants to give her grandmother a grand send off. Money isn't important at a time like this."

"Money is always important," Uncle Albert replied in a lecturing tone. "LaShaun, you need to be careful with mama's estate now. Matter of fact we need to talk about the management of her assets."

"We can talk about it later, Al. Poor kid has

enough on her plate right," Uncle Leo said in a properly solemn tone.

"I didn't arrange for extra deputies," LaShaun murmured. She recognized Chase behind the tinted glass of his windshield and dark sunglasses. The other cruiser took off behind the two motorcycles before she could see the driver.

"Then I wonder why they're here then," Uncle Leo's wife in an uneasy tone. She exchanged a look with Uncle Albert's wife.

"Maybe they're protecting Azalei. I mean that crazy killer is still on the loose," Uncle Albert's wife blurted out. Then blushed at the looks the other women gave her. "I didn't mean to imply…"

"The thing we need to be concerned about is the will. Now LaShaun," Uncle Albert huffed.

"It ain't proper to bring up such matters at my sister's funeral," Great Aunt Geraldine admonished.

"Not now, Albert," Uncle Leo said in a quiet firm tone.

"Humph." Uncle Albert hunched his shoulders as though in pain, sat back in his seat and stared out the window.

The ride to the cemetery took only a few minutes. Cars turned off the paved road down a gravel one leading to the cemetery. Oak and pine trees lined up on either side as they slowly made their way to clearing. The soft crunch of tires on the broken rocks seemed like a signal they were leaving the modern, ordinary world behind them. Limos lined up side-by-side, and family members got out. The other cars parked in haphazard rows. Father Metoyer recited prayers as they eased Monmon Odette's coffin from the hearse. Then the procession went to the graveside. Father Metoyer waited for the family to be seated in a row of folding chairs under a green tent. Most of the crowd from the church spread out behind them. They seemed eager not to miss one second of the infamous Odette Rousselle's farewell.

Once again, LaShaun observed from a distance inside herself. She forgot about her surroundings. Like a slideshow images from her past flashed in her mind: Monmon Odette standing outside in her garden gathering herbs, sunshine making her brown skin glisten; Monmon Odette taking LaShaun to her first day at school; Monmon Odette laughing at reactions of townspeople when she passed them on the street downtown. How she would miss her. LaShaun wondered if anyone other than her felt the loss. Chase stood at the edge of the crowd staring at her. His concern bridged the space separating them.

Father Metoyer performed the brief Rite of Final Commendation. And it was over. The crowd should have dispersed but few left. They seemed to be waiting for the next episode in the Rousselle family drama. As though on cue Brad Gautreau hitched up his holster like a lawman from a B-rated western movie.

Uncle Leo strode out to meet him. "How ya doin, deputy. It was nice of you to come out and give condolences to the family."

Deputy Gautreau looked resolute behind his mirrored sunglasses. "I'm on official business."

"At my mother's funeral services?" Uncle Leo affected an appalled grimace on his broad face. "Sheriff Triche wouldn't allow this kind of disrespect."

"Sheriff Triche ain't in charge, sir." Deputy

Gautreau turned to LaShaun. "You need to come down to the station, *ma'am*."

Savannah made her way through the crowd quickly. "Anything wrong, deputy?"

"Something is about to be set right." Gautreau went over to LaShaun. "You're under arrest for the murder of Rita Rousselle."

Chapter 11

The scene at the sheriff's station had started out routine, at least LaShaun thought so. Everyone else was in an uproar. But LaShaun had faced this kind of questioning in the past. Being plucked from the graveside of her dead grandmother was a creative touch by Deputy Gautreau, but otherwise LaShaun stayed calm. Aunt Leah allowed the private health aide she'd hired to take Azalei home, and gleefully followed the sheriff's department cruisers to the station. Her loud voice could be heard from the lobby proclaiming justice would finally be done. Uncle Leo came in about ten minutes later and Aunt Leah greeted him with a tirade.

"You money grubbing swamp rat," Aunt Leah shouted. "Don't think I haven't figured out why you and Albert are sticking to that girl like glue. You're kissing her butt to get at mama's money." She launched into a string of profanity that turned the air blue.

"Ma'am, you're going to stop kind of talk or I'll personally lock you up for disturbing the peace," Deputy Myrtle Arceneaux said in a measured voice that carried even though she didn't shout.

"I just want to see that murdering little witch locked away so she can't hurt my baby again." Aunt Leah began to bawl and fell against her husband for support.

"Sir, take your wife home," Deputy Arceneaux said to Aunt Leah's husband.

"No, I'm staying right here. This is a public place, and I'm a victim." Aunt Leah shoved her husband away.

"Honey, maybe we ought to leave like the deputy…" He blinked hard and stopped talking when his wife's fiery gaze blistered him.

"I'm not leaving, Henry," Aunt Leah said through clenched teeth.

"Then keep it down. If I hear another outburst you're outta here." Deputy Arceneaux looked at Aunt Leah.

"Yes, ma'am. I have evidence against that heathen," Aunt Leah said. She dramatically pointed at LaShaun.

"Deputy Vincent, take Mrs. Shropshire to an interview room and record her statement." Deputy Arceneaux nodded to a colleague.

"This way, ma'am." The deputy led Aunt Leah and her husband down a hall.

"You come with me." Deputy Gautreau pulled LaShaun by the right arm.

Chase stepped forward. He was on duty and in uniform. "Wait a minute."

"No, you wait a minute. Your judgment in this matter is suspect. So back off. I'm acting chief and that's an order. Or you can be suspended if you like," Gautreau glared at him.

"You have a warrant for her arrest? I haven't seen one yet," Savannah said.

"If she doesn't have anything to hide Miss Rousselle shouldn't mind answering more questions," Gautreau shot back.

"In other words she's not under arrest; which means she can choose not to answer questions. Given the outrageous manner in which she was 'invited' my client will exercise her right to leave. This isn't anything close to what I'd call a reasonable detention." Savannah spoke in a calm tone despite the way the acting sheriff's face grew red with indignation.

District Attorney Hazelton pushed through the glass entrance doors. "What's going on here?"

Tommie Savoie, the mayor, came with him. The town council president brought up the rear. Both politicians frowned at the scene before them. The mayor owned a large grocery store in town. He hated public drama and bad press.

"There are cameras and reporters crawling all over my office saying you went to a funeral to arrest some mourners." The mayor glared at Deputy Gautreau.

"We agreed to handle this situation quietly, with no grandstanding," the council president added. "Remember that discussion when we appointed you to this *temporary* position of authority."

"I'm taking control and getting things done," Acting Chief Gautreau shot back.

"You arrested the woman at her grandmother's funeral in front of three reporters." The council president glared at Gautreau.

"Deputy Arceneaux, please take over while we talk to Brad," The mayor said. He marched off toward the chief's office. The DA nodded for Brad to follow him, and the men disappeared.

"Come to an interview room, if you don't mind," Deputy Arceneaux said to Savannah.

"Thirty minutes, at most, and if the questions aren't new we leave." Savannah nodded to LaShaun who then followed the deputy.

Deputy Arceneaux shook her head at Chase when he started to join them. "We don't want to cause more trouble for this investigation than we've already got."

"Yeah." Chase looked unhappy, but he complied.

After a short walk down two hallways, they settled in the same cheerless interview room LaShaun had been in before. Deputy Arceneaux sat patiently and flipped through a few pages in a thick file. A round clock on the wall loudly ticked off the minutes. Savannah leaned forward and was about to speak when Deputy Arceneaux beat her to it.

"Your cousin Azalei Shropshire hasn't been able to give us much to explain what happened to her or Rita. She does seem terrified when your name is mentioned." Deputy Arceneaux looked at LaShaun steadily. She did not turn when the DA slipped in and quietly shut the interview room door.

"Did she say my client attacked her?" Savannah said.

"No, but the victim's behavior could mean your client was somehow involved."

"She's a traumatized woman whose reactions could mean anything. She didn't act terrified at the funeral with she saw my client. Interview a few people who were there. You can believe I'll get statements." Savannah rested her hands on the top of the metal table between them. "Has Ms. Shropshire been examined by a psychiatrist, and has the psychiatrist made a determination about her mental state?"

Deputy Arceneaux pursed her lips for a few moments. "Yes. She's suffering from posttraumatic stress disorder and memory loss. She could only write notes saying she and Rita went out. Then she veers off into disjointed rambling."

Savannah nodded, and looked at the DA. "I

thought so. If you're through harassing my client, we'll bid the Vermillion Parish Sheriff's Office and its acting boss anything *but* a fond farewell."

Gautreau pushed through the door and brushed past the DA. He held up a cell phone showing a photo. "You wanna explain this?"

"What?" Savannah stared at the phone.

"It's a photo of your client taking a swing at our murder victim." Gautreau squinted at Savannah. "Ms. Shropshire took it, and her mother brought it in."

LaShaun stared at the smart phone's clear picture of her with one hand drawn back to slap Rita. They'd been arguing at Monmon Odette's house only days before Rita and Azalei disappeared.

"We weren't exactly in agreement on the way she handled my grandmother's money, but I didn't kill her." LaShaun stood. For the first time she felt trapped, as though she might lose her freedom.

"This is the smoking gun if you ask me. Shows your client had a violent altercation with our victim, and her alibi is flaky. You're under arrest on suspicion of murder, Miss Rousselle."

"Don't say anything," Savannah said to LaShaun. Then she faced Gautreau. "This so-called smoking gun won't hold up in court."

"You better not count on that," Gautreau shot back. "The jury will be made up of folks with good old common sense. They'll be able to put two and two together, and get a conviction for your client."

Savannah turned to the DA. "You and the mayor better get a grip on your acting Sheriff, or he'll have you in deep legal trouble."

." Gautreau spun to face Hazelton. "We have

enough probable cause to detain her

"The evidence is mounting." Hazelton did not look pleased, or very convinced of his own words.

"C'mon." Gautreau pulled LaShaun from the room.

Savanna followed them out with Hazelton. "You're going to be very sorry you wasted time. Gautreau is not acting rationally, and you know it."

"Our investigation is on-going, but you know very well that your client has the strongest motive." Hazelton replied in a dead tone.

"Very sorry," Savannah repeated with force.

Despite the objections of her attorney, LaShaun was charged and placed in a holding cell. Even Gautreau knew that her bond would be posted quickly. The judge on duty set the amount at a modest fifty thousand dollars. Uncle Leo made the arrangements, and by ten o'clock that night LaShaun was home. Tired, shaken, but at least out of the kind of cell Gautreau wished could be her permanent home. Her uncles wanted to linger and talk, but she managed to get rid of them. Savannah stayed behind.

"God, I'm glad they're gone." LaShaun said when she came back to the living room after locking the front door.

"They're trying to help." Savannah shrugged at the look LaShaun gave her. "Yeah, they really wanted to talk about the estate."

"I'm exhausted and, oh hell." LaShaun groaned when the front door bell rang. "If this is a reporter Gautreau is going to arrest me again for kicking somebody's butt." She marched to the door and jerked the curtain aside before opening it. She groaned again when she saw Chase. After she let him in, he kissed her on the forehead.

"Yes, I know. I should avoid you, and this is a bad idea, blah, blah, blah."

She followed him to the living room. "You must not want to be sheriff, or have any chance at a decent reputation in this town."

"I like enforcing the law and bringing guilty people to justice. Brad doesn't care who goes to jail if it helps him politically. If the public doesn't see that, then they deserve him." Chase waved to Savannah. "Good job, Ms. Attorney."

"I would have earned that compliment if my client hadn't been arrested." Savannah met him in the archway before he could enter the living room. "Stop right there Deputy Broussard. You need to leave."

"I'm not the enemy." Chase frowned at her.

"No, but you'll make defending her more difficult. People will say you're covering for her. The superstitious natives will say she put a spell on you. Trust me there are a lot of them left. We've got enough of a challenge when it comes to public opinion and perception, two things that will help a DA with only circumstantial evidence." Savannah let out a long slow breath. "You care, I get that. But you know I'm right."

"Yeah, I do." Chase's frown relaxed. "Before I go you might be interested in the latest development. The mayor and council rescinded Brad's appointment as acting Sheriff. Myrtle Arceneaux is our acting boss now."

"Ah hell, I wish I could have been there to see Gautreau's expression," Savannah said. She let out a cackle of delight. Then she noticed Chase and LaShaun staring at each other. "Uh, I'll be in the kitchen making us some strong coffee."

Chase stood silently for several long once they were alone minutes. "If you need anything..."

"I'll be fine." LaShaun walked close to him.

"Damn I don't want to walk out of here tonight," Chase said, and put his arms around LaShaun.

"Knowing you believe in me is more than enough."

LaShaun savored the comfort that she would miss all too soon. She buried her face against his chest breathing in the delicious masculine smell of him. A memory that would help her through the long, lonely nights to come.

"Now go," she said softly.

"Okay, but one more thing."

He wrapped both arms around LaShaun and gave her a long, slow kiss. When he finally pulled away, they were both breathless. Chase stepped back and looked at her one last time before he walked out. LaShaun stood shivering from the impact of giving him up. Then she recovered. She locked the front door and went to the kitchen. Savannah sat at the long breakfast bar nibbling a teacake.

"Hope you don't mind. I'm starving."

"I could warm us up something to eat." LaShaun went to the refrigerator and took out a platter of roasted chicken and a large covered bowl of homemade potato salad.

"Don't go to any trouble." Savannah's eyes widened as LaShaun brought out buttered rolls. "But if you insist."

"I'll heat the rolls. The chicken will taste great cold."

"Let me serve myself. You must be worn out,"

Savannah said.

LaShaun waved her back. "I'm okay. Just sit. I have a feeling you've got something you want to tell me, and you didn't want Chase around to hear it."

Savannah sat on the stool again. "So you *are* psychic, and right on the money. There's some real bad stuff going on around here."

"You mean worse than one cousin getting her tongue cut off, and another cousin turning up dead? If there is then I haven't heard about it." LaShaun put the rolls in the microwave and set the timer.

"I hired an investigator to dig around. Rita and Azalei were keeping bad company, just like Rita's mama said. They were partying hard and throwing around cash. Some wild private parties have been going on around here. They say Quentin Trosclair financed the good times. Lots of liquor, drugs and sex." Savannah shook her head.

"Quentin always loved exotic good times." LaShaun crossed her arms.

"So I've heard." Savannah cleared her throat and raised her eyebrows.

"Chase knows about Quentin and me. Well, not all of the details. But enough to know I'm no angel." LaShaun shrugged.

"Okay." Savannah digested that news for a few seconds then went on. "Quentin is backing Gautreau for sheriff, but keeping it quiet. But, this is the thing that only a couple of people were brave enough to even whisper; Gautreau has been to a few of these private parties. He's got a healthy campaign fund from his party 'friends'. Some of them include business folks looking to locate to this area, and get lucrative contracts.'"

The microwave timer dinged and LaShaun took out the steaming rolls. She brought Savannah a plate of food. "Azalei and Rita must have been in on some juicy secrets."

"Maybe, but I don't need know those juicy secrets. Just having this information means I can make a nice case for reasonable doubt." Savannah smiled as though looking forward to facing Hazelton. She ate a forkful of potato salad and sighed. "You should eat something."

"I can't," LaShaun said and pushed the food away.

The thought of eating twisted her stomach into a knot. While Savannah enjoyed the down home feast, LaShaun went to the bay window and looked out into the dark. She could only imagine the terror Rita and Azalei suffered that night. LaShaun shivered at the evil that must be inside a man to strike out in such vicious way. Or was it at the hands of a man? As she concentrated hard on that question, LaShaun focused on dense black shadow of trees at the edge of manicured lawn. The bright security lamp did not touch the dense darkness of the woods; just as compassion or goodness did not touch the thing that had maimed one woman and killed another without mercy. After a few seconds, a blue vapor glowed. LaShaun blinked to see if she was dreaming. The light wrapped around a huge oak tree like a vine. No, like a snake. Savannah's voice sounded distant.

"That was some delicious. Thanks for the food. Look, don't be too concerned about what the DA thinks. His so-called theory of the crime is of full of holes. A revocable trust is a done deal. Your grandmother had already given you the assets. Rita and

Azalei had more of a motive to come after *you* than you had to harm them."

"Yeah, right," LaShaun said without taking her gaze from the woods.

"You shouldn't worry, okay? The DA has a steep hill to climb, and you better believe he knows it."

LaShaun gasped when she realized Savannah was standing next to her. She took Savannah by the arm and pulled her from the window. "Thanks for everything, Savannah. You've been great through all this, but you must be tired. I'm sure your husband is worried about you being out so late. Go home and get some rest."

"Are you rushing me out of here because of my welfare, or do you have another reason?" Savannah craned her neck to look over LaShaun's shoulder to the window.

"What are you talking about?" LaShaun tensed.

"I'm talking about that good looking deputy. This isn't the time for romantic interludes on the bayou." Savannah shook a finger close to LaShaun's nose.

"I agree completely," LaShaun said. "And if he shows up I'm going to send him packing. Girl Scout's honor."

"You were never a Girl Scout. You told us scary stores until we refused to go camping in the woods, drove the troop leaders nuts." Savannah gave a short laugh. She picked up her purse, but still didn't move to leave. "You're right about Paul. He's sent me three text messages in the last hour. Now remember what I said."

"About what?" LaShaun tried not to let her impatience show through.

"Hazelton has a shaky case, so don't stay up all night worrying."

"I'm not going to be thinking about the DA tonight, trust me." LaShaun resisted the urge to shove Savannah to the front door. She walked behind her giving token answers to Savannah's talk about their next move and doing more investigation.

"Wait a minute. I don't think you should be out here by yourself," Savannah stood in the open front door. She looked around at the rural setting, and the dark night.

"I've got strong locks and a big shotgun in a closet. Drive carefully." LaShaun gently pushed her forward onto the porch.

"Okay. Anyway I have a feeling Deputy Broussard is not far away." Savannah winked at LaShaun. "Goodnight."

"Goodnight," LaShaun repeated. She watched as Savannah got into her Buick Enclave and drove off. "I hope she's wrong about Chase being around here."

When the red taillights disappeared, LaShaun spun around and ran down the hallway. Then she remembered the front door was still open. She went back to secure it then went to her grandmother's bedroom. The old diary lay open on the dresser. LaShaun picked it up slowly, holding her breath for a long minute before exhaling. Chase could arrest a human killer, and with his strong arms could overpower a physical opponent. Savannah could use her intelligence and skill to defend LaShaun in a court of law. But LaShaun had to face this unearthly threat on her own.

The pages no longer had a faded aged appearance in the soft yellow light coming from the table lamps in the room. Strangely, the ink looked fresh as though the words had been written only days or hours before instead of generations ago. LaShaun felt compelled to rush to the woods, but the words of her ancestors told her to wait. LaShaun looked up from the pages and sighed. She put the diary aside and picked up another one. The wind outside picked up until it made a sharp whistling sound. She went to the window that faced the woods. The blue light still curled around the trunk of a giant live oak, an invitation. No, more like a challenge. LaShaun cleared the antique table. She found a lace runner and three white candles in brass holders on it. LaShaun brought out the large ornate Bible she'd found in Monmon Odette's antique armoire. It had passed from hand to hand since 1902, and used on formal family occasions. Holding Monmon Odette's treasured rosary beads, she got on her knees before the flicker candles and began to pray. Windows rattled in the old house. The longer the prayed the louder the wind moaned outside. Creaks and snaps crackled as the wooden frame of her grandmother's large Creole-styled home resisted the pressure of a strange force.

"Enough." LaShaun stood.

All noise ceased, like the quiet after a tempest. Yet, LaShaun knew very well that she was still in a hurricane. This peace was only the eye of the storm passing over. More was to come. She looked out into the night. A full smoky yellow moon stood above the trees. LaShaun left the bedroom and went down the hall past the kitchen and out of the back door.

"I knew you'd come."

The throaty whisper gave her chills, but LaShaun didn't answer in words. Instead, she crossed the boundary of light and entered a darkness that seemed to beckon. The blue light danced crazily in the distance, a clearing she knew well. When she got to the edge of the trees shadows seemed to move around her. LaShaun fought the urge to run.

"You'd just pull me back, wouldn't you?" LaShaun said to the air around her.

The reply was snapping of branches that sounded like a dozen insane gremlins giggling. She gasped when a pressure in the middle of her back forced her forward two steps. Monmon Odette's words came to her clearly.

"Cher, you must go on your own. Be bold."

This was advice she'd given to LaShaun as a child while taught to practice the old religion their ancestors brought from Saint-Domingue. LaShaun nodded as though her grandmother stood next to her. She clutched Monmon Odette's rosary, and shook herself like a prizefighter about to enter the ring. Then she walked straight for the family cemetery. A faint shape, no more than a translucent outline, stood next to the oldest headstone.

"In the name of the most powerful one and only God, I pray that this doorway be slammed shut on the wicked ones who bring destruction to us."

LaShaun spoke calmly in spite of the way her heart hammered. The shape seemed to cock its head to one side. Then raucous laughter bounced from tree trunk to tree trunk about her. She fingered the gold cross over her heart. Laughter turned to a guttural growl that filled her ears. Pressure pushed her until she dropped to her knees and went forward into a crouch. Obscenities slapped her from all sides, and her legs pried apart by something hard and hot. Fighting the terror that tore through her, LaShaun started to pray.

Invisible fingers pulled at the crotch of her jeans, and roughly caressed her breasts, but she continued to pray. Warmth flowed down her chin. She realized her nose was bleeding. Panic made her tremble violently, and she dropped the cross. More laughter assaulted her as a gust of wind blew dust in her eyes. The darkness thickened until she felt smothered. Moonlight lit the ground as leaves parted in the wind. LaShaun clawed through earth and grass for the glitter of gold until she found it. She prayed, screaming the words of faith. Hours passed, but gradually like a balloon losing air the tumult died away.

Exhausted, LaShaun panicked for few moments when she couldn't muster the strength to get up. Somehow, she managed to half crawl out of the woods toward the circle of brightness around the house. After a few steps, her legs gave out and she curled into a ball on the ground. She lay on the grass physically drained, but free of the evil spirit that wanted to control of her mind and body.

She lost track of time, but finally got to her feet and staggered into the house.

When she pushed through the back door her great-great grandmother's clock chimed the fourth hour of April twenty-fourth. The time and date Odette Marie Hypolite Rousselle was born, the seventh daughter of a seventh daughter.

Chapter 12

At the arraignment the small courtroom was packed. LaShaun's family split along the two rows of benches. Her uncles and a handful of cousins sat behind LaShaun and Savannah at the defense desk. Aunt Leah sat with a boisterous contingent of relatives who showed up to give her support. Reporters were scattered throughout the crowd on both sides of the courtroom. LaShaun looked back, surprised to see Azalei seated between Aunt Leah and a scowling woman, one of Aunt Leah's best friends. Azalei looked less dazed, but still did not seem interested in what was going on around her. Aunt Leah gave LaShaun a fierce glare. Shaken by the poison in her dark eyes, LaShaun looked away just as the Judge Alsace Trahan strode in.

"You see. She can't even look us in the eye. She knows what she's done, and I'm going to see she pays for it," Aunt Leah said.

Murmurs of agreement rose around her like a cloud of buzzing insects. The relatives sitting on LaShaun's side of the gallery tossed out a few comments in response. The click of cameras responded as well so the reporters could catch the reactions on both sides.

Judge Trahan stopped flipping through the pages in front of him, picked up the gavel, and banged it. The sound brought everyone to attention. "Let me make this clear, I won't put up with outbursts or a lot of noise. I can and will clear everybody out of here if necessary." He looked around. "As for you reporters, no snapping pictures once proceedings begin. This is a preliminary hearing, not a reality show. I won't repeat myself.

Proceed Mr. Hazelton."

"Your honor, the state has provided the court with evidence that Ms. Rousselle had an on-going, bitter and even sometimes violent feud with the victims in this case. We have pictures of one such fight, and the police reports detailing a disturbance involving the defendant and the victims. Ms. Rousselle attacked one or both of the victims on both occasions. The cause of the animosity was quite familiar, money. The victims had strong reason to believe that the defendant had taken advantage of their ailing grandmother so she could take control of a valuable estate. The defendant has a questionable alibi for the projected time of these crimes." Hazelton wore a solemn expression as he approached the bench. "Not to mention she has a history of being involved in another murder trial--"

"Objection." Savannah shot from her chair. "Mr. Hazelton knows very well that those charges were never brought, and my client was only questioned. He is attempting to create a hostile and prejudicial climate for my client."

"Sustained." Judge Trahan's thick dark brown eyebrows bunched together as he looked at the DA. "You know better. Don't bring that other matter up again."

"Yes, your honor. I only intended to establish the reckless nature and tendency toward violence of this defendant. We think there is more than enough evidence to support going forward with a trial." Hazelton sat down. His assistant seated next to him nodded as though she thought the decision was clear.

"Ms. Honoré." Judge Trahan nodded to Savannah.

She stood, smoothed down the front of her dark

gray suit jacket, and then walked a few steps forward. "Your honor, the defense does not intend to dispute the facts of the family conflict between Ms. Rousselle and the victims. What Mr. Hazleton didn't mention was that Mrs. Odette Rousselle had created a revocable trust that effectively transferred all of the assets to my client immediately upon her death. So, my client didn't have a financial motive to harm the victims. She owns the properties and monies in the estate outright. In addition, I can call witnesses who will say that the victims struck out at my client for that very reason. Most importantly, there is no physical evidence linking my client to the crime. Even the surviving victim has not once accused her. We also have information that because of their lifestyles and questionable associates, both victims could have been attacked for reasons that have nothing to do with the estate of the late Mrs. Rousselle. In short, this is a hurried case thrown together based on old gossip and incomplete police work." Savannah sat down.

"I see you both have witness testimony," Judge Trahan rumbled.

"Yes," Savannah replied quickly with a confident nod.

"Yes, sir." Hazelton stood.

"You first, Mr. Hazleton."

"I call Mrs. Leah Shropshire to the stand," the DA said.

Aunt Leah patted Azalei on the shoulder, whispered something to her other daughter then marched forward. Hazelton opened the short wooden door of the bar separating the lawyers from the gallery. She managed to give Savannah a contemptuous glare as she walked by. Aunt Leah sat down after being sworn in.

"Mrs. Shropshire, were you present to see the animosity between your daughter, Ms. Rita Rousselle and the defendant?"

"I certainly was, like most of my family. The ones that have the decency to be honest." Aunt Leah glared at her brothers.

"Just stick to what you know ma'am," Judge Trahan said. He shot a warning look at the spectators and the rising murmurs died away.

"Yes, sir. I was present when LaShaun went after her own cousins like a crazy person. She tried to choke the life out of poor Rita. My daughter showed me the pictures so she can't deny it." Aunt Leah turned her furious gaze on Savannah. "

"That's all. Thank you." Hazelton sat down.

"Mrs. Shropshire, has your daughter been able to tell you what happened?" Savannah stood, but didn't walk toward the witness stand.

Aunt Leah squinted at Savannah. "Of course not. She's too traumatized, not to mention your client tried to cut off her tongue completely. Thank God she wasn't successful, but not because LaShaun didn't try. But the doctors say she'll heal and with speech therapy..."

"Your honor, please instruct the witness to answer the questions only," Savannah said calmly as though she didn't notice Aunt Leah's belligerence.

"Mrs. Shropshire, you can't make accusations. Stick to a subject at hand." Judge Trahan gazed at Aunt Leah.

"Fine," she snapped. "No, Azalei hasn't been able to talk."

"Has she mentioned my client at all in connection to what happened to her, or to the other victim?" Savannah pressed.

Aunt Leah looked away from Savannah. "No. But that doesn't mean…"

"That's all. Thank you." Savannah sat down.

"Your honor, I direct you to the copies of other witnesses we have listed that can verify the on-going hostility Ms. Rousselle showed toward the victims. We believe there is enough evidence to have a trial." Hazelton stood as though waiting for the ruling.

Savannah's paralegal came down the center aisle of the gallery quickly, leaned over the bar. and whispered to her. Then he handed her a folder.

"Your honor, I have a witness, Mr. Jerry Garland, that we were only just able to locate," Savannah said.

"Objection, your honor. We haven't reviewed information from this witness." Hazelton looked at his young assistant who shook her head and shrugged. Then she started flipping through a file in front of her.

"We weren't sure we would be able to find him, or if it would affect my client's right to self-incrimination," Savannah said. "But we did list his name in the documents as a possible witness sent to the DA's office, your honor."

"I'll allow it." Judge Trahan leaned forward on both elbows as though intrigued.

"The defense calls Jerry Garland to the stand." Savannah crossed her arms as the man came forward.

LaShaun shivered as she recognized him as one of the men that had attacked her in the woods. Chase had supplied names and details of the incident. Jerry Garland was dressed in a plaid shirt and dark pants. He had combed his hair, and his clothes looked fairly clean. Yet, he still had a scruffy, unkempt air about him. He did not seem happy to be present, or to be swearing an oath to tell the truth. He mumbled his "Yes" response to tell the truth, and managed to make it seem Savannah would have to pull it out of him by force.

"Mr. Garland, were you near Bayou Teche between the hours of nine and eleven on the morning on April seventh?" Savannah looked at papers in her hand. She seemed to hold them up to make sure he saw them.

"Far as I can remember." Garland rubbed his jaw.

"Did you see my client on that day?" Savannah continued to look down.

He looked as LaShaun did his gaze slid back to Savannah. "Yeah."

"Were you alone when you met her in a clearing about a half mile from the roadway?"

Jerry twisted in his chair and cleared his throat. "No, I was with a buddy of mine."

"Were you and this buddy there by accident?" Savannah looked up at him. She took a step forward.

"Uh, nope. We, uh, followed her out there that day." Jerry's eyes shifted to the judge then back to Savannah.

"Isn't it true that someone hired you to follow Ms. Rousselle with the intention of intimidating her, and in fact you came close to sexually assaulting her?" Savannah's voice cracked like a whip at the man.

"Well, I wouldn't say all that now."

"I have a statement from a deputy, Mr. Garland. Don't perjure yourself," Savannah said.

"We got a little rough with her. Rita told me,

Azalei, and her friends said she was a trouble maker that needed a little nudge to maybe get out of town." Jerry cleared his throat.

"Oh really?" Savannah looked at the DA and his assistant then turned back to him. "How do you know Ms. Shropshire and Rita Rousselle?"

"We're friends like," Jerry said, and shrugged.

"That's a filthy lie," Aunt Leah blurted out. Several of the cousins with her began talking loudly.

"Quiet. Bailiff, escort those folks out of my courtroom," Judge Trahan barked.

There was a moment of disruption as two husky officers went to that side of the gallery. Aunt Leah huffed and puffed, and several of LaShaun's cousins argued, but the court officers shushed them and herded the group out. Aunt Leah took Azalei with her. When the two officers returned, Judge Trahan nodded to Savannah.

"In fact, you and the victims partied together where there was a lot of drinking. In a few instances there may have been drugs on the premises," Savannah said.

"I don't know nothin' about drugs being around," Garland said quickly shaking his head. "I heard some rumors about ecstasy and stuff being passed around. Some of them girls were wild." He grinned and turned to the judge. When Judge Trahan scowled at him the grin vanished.

"So it's your testimony that Ms. Shropshire and Ms. Rita Rousselle associated with drug users and dealers." Savannah ignored the hum this caused from the spectators. The judge tapped his gavel and got silence again. "Isn't it also true that some prominent local citizens frequented these wild parties?"

Garland's facial muscles tensed. He glanced around the courtroom and cleared his throat. "We had some pretty big parties. Coulda been anybody there."

"So any of those people might not be thrilled if either Ms. Shropshire or Ms. Rousselle mentioned their names? Isn't that right?"

"I dunno," Garland muttered. He fidgeted in his seat and tugged at his collar. Then he leaned forward to speak into the microphone. "I just went to the parties to have a good time. I didn't see nobody sell or use drugs. I don't know nothin' about no illegal activity." He blushed when snickers of disbelief came from all sides of the courtroom.

"So Ms. Shropshire wanted you to intimidate Ms. Rousselle, is that right?"

"Yeah."

"Did she pay you?" Savannah raised an eyebrow when he hesitated. "You're under oath."

"Yeah."

"Didn't you disagree about the payment because she thought you'd failed? On the other hand you wanted extra money because the job hadn't been so easy." Savannah drove home the words like nails in Garland's coffin.

"No, that's not what we got into a fuss about. And I didn't try to rape nobody," Garland blurted out angrily.

Savannah pounced. "But you admit that you quarreled with the victims. It could be argued that you had a motive to harm them."

"What? No, that's not what I meant to say. I refuse to answer on the grounds it might incriminate me." Garland wiped beads of sweat from his forehead.

"You've said more than enough," Savannah shot

back. She gave the DA and his assistant a razor thin smile as she sat down. "I'm through with this witness."

Hazelton strode forward with a look of barely contained rage on his face. He sliced a glance to his right where Deputy Gautreau stood. He got a defiant gaze tossed right back for his effort. Then the DA stared at Chase, who stood behind the last row of benches against the wall. Chase exited quickly before his presence could become the focus of attention. Hazelton smoothed down his tie as though trying to contain his frustration. His expression was composed when he faced Garland.

"Mr. Garland, were you threatened in anyway by a member of law enforcement? You've made some statements that could put you in legal hot water. I'm wondering why you'd do that?" Hazelton turned to face the gallery.

Garland rubbed his hands together. "I got picked up on some charges in Orleans Parish. They'll cut me a break for being a good citizen." His last words brought a few chuckles from the spectators.

"Right, a good citizen." Hazelton went to his table and sat down. "That's all."

Garland scurried from the witness chair and out of the courtroom, head down and obviously happy to be leaving. Aunt Leah's supporters hissed at him. A few of them tossed heated comments about his character, but low enough not to attract the Judge Trahan's attention from looking over his notes.

Savannah stood. "Your honor, I contend that to say the investigation of these crimes is incomplete is a gross understatement. The state should not rush to trial on this matter. The victims deserve nothing less than a thorough and totally unbiased look at all possible suspects."

"Despite theatrics more appropriate for a second rate soap opera the facts remain the same. Ms. Rousselle had the only well-documented motive to commit these crimes. She attacked both witnesses in the past, and she has no alibi for the time of crimes." Hazelton stood straight.

"The time of the attacks hasn't been definitively established, and the district attorney knows that very well." Savannah was about to go on but stopped when Judge Trahan raised a hand.

"I'm going to take this matter under advisement. Court is adjourned." Judge Trahan gathered up his files, nodded to the two court bailiffs, and left the bench. The officers went to opposite ends of the courtroom and herded out the gaggle of spectators who wanted to linger.

"What does that mean?" LaShaun put a hand on Savannah's arm.

"It means I've given him a lot more to think about than he expected. So much for the DA's open and shut case for a trial."

"You did a fantastic job, boss." Savannah's paralegal grinned at her.

"Your investigation skills helped. You'll be another Magnum PI before long." Savannah winked at him.

"Who?" Jarius blinked at her.

"Thanks for making me feel very old. Never mind. You've earned an extra afternoon off." Savannah smiled at him.

"Shoot, I'm not ready to take off early yet. The

action is way too interesting.

"Interesting is not the word I would use. But you're right to use the present tense. We're not out of the woods yet," Savannah replied.

LaShaun shivered at her reference to woods. "You're so right."

"You okay?" Savannah put a hand on her shoulder.

"Sure." LaShaun stood. "So what's next?"

"We wait for the judge to decide if there is enough evidence against you for a trial. In the meantime having the real perpetrator dragged kicking and screaming into the sheriff's station would help." Savannah sighed and shook her head.

"I'm working on it. I didn't know there were so many rocks to turn over in little old sleepy Beau Chene." The paralegal shook his head.

"You have no idea," LaShaun said quietly.

Savannah let out a long sigh. "Well, troops, time to go home and gird our loins for the next battle."

"I'm ready, general." Jarius grinned at her and saluted.

As they walked from the courtroom, Savannah and Jarius talked legal strategy in a relaxed way. They seemed encouraged. LaShaun knew there was more to come. The next battle would be spiritual warfare. Her night in the woods had only been the opening shot. The diaries warned that the loa, once awakened, would not simply slink away. After all, he'd been with her family for over a hundred years. Its hunger for power and devotion to chaos knew no bounds.

* * *

Two days later Judge Trahan made his decision. He informed District Attorney Hazelton there wasn't enough convincing evidence to take LaShaun to trial. The case, he said in a dark tone, had reasonable doubt stamped all over it. Hazelton took the news with grace while he was in the judge's office. He didn't hold his temper when he got Brad Gautreau into his office according town gossip.

Meanwhile the media had a great time describing every salacious detail of Beau Chene's secret underbelly. Headlines like, "Sleepy Bayou Town Has Dirty Little Secrets" sent the mayor into a public rant. Reporters circled around town like flies going from one pile of manure to another, delighted to sniff out more muck.

That night LaShaun sat on her front porch rocking back and forth at a lazy pace. Waiting in the shadows. She'd called her Aunt Leah to come out for a meeting. Aunt Leah balked and retorted she had no intention of meeting with a murderer miles from help. When LaShaun suggested she bring Deputy Gautreau for protection, Aunt Leah cursed for a good thirty seconds then slammed down the phone. No matter. LaShaun knew her message would reach the right person.

LaShaun called to give Quentin a personal invitation. Hearing from LaShaun not only stroked his ego, but also incited his insatiable need for scandalous thrills. Quentin wasn't afraid. On the contrary, he reacted as if LaShaun had invited him to a party. He even offered to bring wine and some of the best marijuana in south Louisiana.

Finally, LaShaun called Chase. He vehemently

objected, calling her plan both dangerous and foolish. When LaShaun told him she'd already invited the other players in this drama, Chase swore and agreed to be there, but on his conditions. LaShaun agreed to his strategy to minimize the risk of someone else getting killed, as Chase put it. Still she knew he could only deal with the human side of this risky equation. She only hoped and prayed that she had adequately prepared for the unworldly threat.

The antique clock chimed the hour. Twelve times the bells tolled to announce midnight. Inside the house was dark except for one small lamp. LaShaun had considered turning off the large security lamp in the yard, but Chase put his foot down on that point. She worried that the light would keep away a less substantial visitor, she need to deal with him and whatever control he'd taken in these events. Or maybe he had gained more strength than she knew. LaShaun was in uncharted waters. In the last thirteen hours, she had read all ten of Monmon Odette's diaries, back to the very first one when she was only a girl of twelve. Still LaShaun wasn't tired. Instead she felt a kind of energy, a tingling in her body like an electrical charge as though she'd tapped into a strange energy source. The young Odette had used her gifts to summon the loa; little realizing she was only reawakening the same spirit her ancestors had called on. But tonight wasn't about the past. LaShaun had a duty to carry out.

Headlights swung around the corner from the road. Tires crunched on gravel as the sports car slowed to a stop. The driver's door swung open and the interior light blinked on then quickly extinguished. The figure stayed outside the ring of illumination cast by the large security light in the yard. The person stood for a few minutes observing LaShaun. Then the car door slammed shut.

LaShaun stopped the motion of the rocking chair. "Hello, Azalei. I see you've made a rapid recovery."

Chapter 13

"Lucky thing you only sliced the side of my tongue when you attacked me. I'm still in shock." Azalei spoke with a slight lisp. She mimicked the slouched posture and vacant stare she'd worn in court. Seconds later she laughed and straightened up.

"You've got that act down pat, huh?" LaShaun stood.

"Hell yeah. Of course, it helps that folks *want* to believe you're guilty of something. You have a well documented history of violence." Azalei gave a laughed harder. She remained just outside the wide ring of light cast from the overhead security lamp.

A second set of headlights appeared. Even the nighttime didn't dim the gleam of the shiny white Lexus SUV. When it came to a stop there was no movement for several minutes. Azalei gazed at it expectantly then looked back at the porch. The window on the driver's side slide down silently but Quentin didn't get out. Even in the dark LaShaun could feel his arrogant amusement across the yards separating them.

"Took you long enough to get here," Azalei called to him. "I don't have time for games."

"When do you have time for games, Azalei?" LaShaun stood and walked to the edge of the porch. "Maybe the night you helped that swamp snake torture and kill Rita?"

"But everybody knows you killed Rita, LaShaun. The sheriff just spent the last day searching Monmon's property. I would say your property, but it won't be once you're locked up." Azalei sounded confident, her voice strong.

"That right, Quentin? You helped Azalei engineer all this to get your hands on Monmon Odette's property." LaShaun looked at her cousin again. "He'll end up with everything. Then he'll toss you overboard."

Quentin sat in the Lexus, he seemed content to stay where he was and observe. A flame appeared as he lit a slender cigar. He puffed until the end glowed red, and the flame from the lighter went out again. If he was worried, Quentin didn't show it. He seemed at ease several miles from the next few houses scattered along Rousselle Lane.

"Stupid bitch. You think it's just about the money," Azalei said. She glanced at the Lexus as though looking for some support. When no sign came from Quentin Azalei scowled at him.

"That's the first sign you're on your own," LaShaun said.

Azalei turned back toward the porch and walked closer to it. "I don't need him or anybody else to handle my business. Unlike most of Beau Chene, I'm not scared of you, LaShaun. Not even a little bit."

"Then you're more of a stupid bitch than I am, because I'm gonna send you to prison. Right after I whip your silly ass." LaShaun came down the steps at a leisurely pace and closed the distance between them. "Poor Rita underestimated how lowdown and sneaky you can be. She was too trusting." LaShaun's voice broke as she spoke of her cousin.

"Don't get too sentimental about 'poor' Rita, sugar. She was ready to plant a knife in your back to get Monmon's estate." Azalei wore a nasty grin.

"You played on her insecurity and childhood

resentment, didn't you?" LaShaun balled both of her hands into fists. "I'll bet you were very patient at rubbing her wounds with salt."

"It wasn't hard. The old lady made it so obvious you were the golden child in this family. Rita knew that like the rest of us."

"So you pulled her into your grimy little schemes. Then you played a trump card and got Quentin to romance her. What happened? Did Rita find out that it was all a set up?" LaShaun asked.

"Speaking of stupid, she actually thought Quentin was in love with her. Unfortunately, she got a conscience when we started doing some serious business deals. I just needed the investment capital and --"

"Shut the hell up," Quentin drawled from the Lexus. He finally got out of the SUV. "Your big mouth got us into this mess."

Azalei spun around. "Correction, your sleazy sexual habits and slimy friends got us into this. I tried to tell you hiring that trailer park trash to deal with LaShaun was a bad idea."

Quentin surprised both women by laughing. He walked past Azalei toward LaShaun. "I have no idea what she's talking about, sweetie."

"I hope you don't think he's in love with you," LaShaun retorted.

"Quentin is in love with power and money, in that order. He'll stay with me as long as I have both," Azalei replied and tossed her long auburn weave.

"Rita found out Quentin was sleeping with you, too, and that she'd had been used. Once Rita realized what scum you both are she decided not to play your game. So she had to die."

LaShaun forced herself to unclench her hands. The tension and wrath coursing through her would weaken her focus. A flash of light to her left came from deep within the woods. Was the loa here with them? She fingered the gris-gris in her left hand and recited one of the short prayers an ancestor had written in her journal.

"C'mon. Taking you down is turning out to be too easy." Azalei threw back her head and laughed. "Your poor innocent Rita tried to blackmail Quentin into letting her in on some of his business deals. Being greedy and dumb is a fatal combination."

"More motive. Just keep talking, cousin. Dig that hole deeper." LaShaun saw another movement to her left. "But who attacked you? That's what I don't understand."

Azalei lost the look of boldness for the first time. "Something happened that night. Those fools were supposed to go after Rita, mess her up. Not kill her and attack me. They started off following the script, then they snapped."

"Are you sure your boyfriend didn't decide to get rid of two problems in one night?" LaShaun felt a familiar tingle. She got flashes of insight. Then she studied the spooked expression Azalei wore. "Those two are sleaze bags, but they're also cowards. Someone told them they had to do more than rough you and Rita up. Did you even see who knocked you out that night?"

"Cut the bull, LaShaun. Your days of being Miss It are over." Azalei's eyes narrowed.

LaShaun gave a short, contemptuous laugh. "That's what I thought. Jerry and his stupid pal ran off. When you woke up was he there? I'll bet there was a mist all around and you felt a chill. But he convinced you that he'd come in time to save you, didn't he? Said he had a feeling Jerry and his friend couldn't be trusted to do the right thing."

"How'd you know? Wait a minute. Don't try that voodoo hoodoo ghost story shit on me. You and Monmon Odette might have fooled everybody else, but the family knows it's all a bunch of fake crap." Azalei started at a night sound. She looked around her sharply, as though noticing for the first time that she was way out in the country at night.

"He came to make sure you were both dead, but you hid thinking it was Jerry coming back. I'll bet Quentin was stunned when you got in touch with him." LaShaun glanced back and forth between them.

"This little play has been almost amusing to watch, but let's get down to business," Quentin said. He dropped the cigar and ground it into the gravel with one heel. "Sorry, but there's too much at stake to let you go running around telling wild stories."

"You can't really believe I'd bring you out here and not have back up," LaShaun said calmly.

"You're the one left hanging, LaShaun. Your man Broussard is probably somewhere hoping his chances to get elected aren't completely shot," Azalei said.

"No, ma'am, actually I'm right here. I arrived just in time to hear every last word." Chase stepped from the shadows. He'd been hiding on the far side of the porch around the west corner of the house.

"Too bad nobody will listen, Deputy Broussard," Azalei spat. "Your credibility will be zero once everyone knows you're banging the voodoo queen."

"You could be right." Chase kept his calm southern

gentleman tone. "But even a rural sheriff's department is high tech these days."

Azalei looked at Quentin. Her smile froze. "What are you talking about?"

"I carry a video camera in my cruiser. These little things fit in the palm of my hand. But I can also mount them anywhere." Chase swept out one arm. "Try to guess where it is."

"That's a pretty pitiful bluff," Azalei said. Still her gaze darted at the darkness.

"Smile for the camera, cousin," LaShaun replied.

A powerful motor rumbled as headlights swung around. The newcomer pulled up beneath a swath of light from the huge lamp behind Monmon Odette's house. A Vermillion Parish sheriff's department cruiser parked beside the Lexus. Deputy Gautreau emerged with a nine millimeter Glock in his hand. LaShaun heard Chase let out a soft hiss.

"Glad you got here, buddy. I know who killed Rita. I've got it all recorded." Chase didn't move toward his colleague despite his words. "So that means everything has changed.

"You're right, bro. Things have definitely changed. Throw your gun over here, and move slow so I don't think you're going to shoot me. Do it now." Gautreau pointed the gun at LaShaun's head.

When Chase tossed the gun away, Quentin retrieved it and walked over to stand next to Gautreau. "You didn't really think I'd come out here with no back-up did you?"

"My cousin lured me out here saying she just wanted to talk, to make peace. Instead she attacked me again forcing Deputy Gautreau to shoot her and her lover," Azalei said, her voice shaking. Then she smiled. "That's exactly what I'm going to tell the DA and the media. I might even get a made for TV movie deal out of this, along with Monmon Odette's estate. I don't have to share it with anybody now that 'poor' Rita is gone."

"You really think these two will let you leave here still breathing, Azalei? They didn't want to share the goodies with Rita. What makes you different?" LaShaun nodded toward the two men.

"Nice try, LaShaun. They both know I have the keys to every closet that hides their skeletons," Azalei tossed back.

"Exactly," Quentin snapped.

He walked over to Azalei and shoved her hard. She went flying, and then stumbled. She found her footing, but also ended up closer to LaShaun and Chase than her conspirators. When she started toward Quentin, he aimed Chase's gun at her.

"You're so right, baby. Being greedy and dumb is a lethal combination." Quentin grinned at her.

"They're going to toss you into the bayou and let the gators take care of the evidence. Right, Quentin? Of course, you tried that with your grandfather, and they found him too soon. Or maybe even the gators didn't like the taste of a putrid Trosclair." LaShaun tried to keep the attention on her as Chase inched to a thick gardenia bush.

"I always loved that wicked tongue of yours." Quentin smacked his lips and winked at her.

LaShaun stared at her former lover with disgust. "What did I ever see in you?"

"The same thing your cousins saw, darlin'. Money,

influence, and some of the hottest sex you'll ever get. You know, I envy you, Chase. LaShaun is one sweet piece." Quentin looked at Chase steadily as he spoke. "I'd give you x-rated details, Deputy Broussard, but we've got more important business right now."

Chase snarled at him. "You're a high-class of piece of trash."

"Don't move, man, or I'll drop you right here and now." Gautreau pointed the Glock at Chase. The red laser point landed on Chase's chest. "Clear shot."

"Don't be a fool, Brad. These two killed Rita, and I've got it on tape," Chase said. "You could still cut a deal. I think they pulled you into something darker than you knew how to handle."

"Oh, I know how to handle it all right. We just gotta clean up loose ends. I can have it all." Gautreau replied with a frown.

Quentin shook his head no. "Just shut up, and let's get on with it. We've got to find that dash cam he's got hidden around here.

"We'll have time to look when it gets light," Brad replied without taking his gaze or gun off Chase. "First things we dump the garbage."

"More than one video cam, fellas," Chase called out. "So, Brad. You're in this whole dirty deal, huh?"

"Brad is definitely involved up to his thick neck, maybe he planned it all. You're not as dense as you look. Quentin, you'll have to watch your back for a long, long time." LaShaun tried to distract them from Chase again.

"Your concern warms my heart. But don't worry, sweetie. I'll be just fine." Quentin walked around as casually as he spoke, as though he had no care at all.

"Too bad you and your cousins got into it over money. Tragic, all three of you dying because of greed," Gautreau said.

"Quentin, baby, c'mon. My grandmother's property will most likely come to me." Azalei's voice cracked with desperation. "Remember all those shale formations and the millions we'll get from natural gas?"

"My lawyers tell me your grandmother didn't make sure she had clear ownership of the mineral rights. So I don't need *you,*" Quentin replied.

"Explaining two dead women and a dead fellow deputy is going to be tough even for you, Brad," Chase said.

"I'll manage. The Rousselle family doesn't exactly have the best reputation, and your questionable behavior getting involved with a suspect will round out the story nicely," Brad said. "Now move away from that bush or I'll start by shooting your woman in the gut. That's a slow painful way to die."

Azalei let out a series of terrified squeaks before she was able to speak. "Quentin, please. I can still be of use to you. I'll confirm any story y'all tell about LaShaun and Broussard. That will make it more believable. "

"I have no reason to trust you. Maybe you'll decide to blackmail me the way Rita tried," Quentin replied.

"I kept a file," Azalei shouted. "My mother will know where to look if anything happens to me."

"Where are those sex videos of us, Azalei? I might let you go if you give them to me," Brad barked. "And I doubt seriously you'd leave those anywhere for your mother to find."

Azalei sneered when LaShaun shot a look of

contempt in her direction. "Don't get self-righteous, LaShaun. Not after the way you used your body to get what you want. Obviously Deputy Broussard is under that same spell."

Quentin laughed. "You're not even close to being in LaShaun's league. You're a lucky man, Broussard. Excuse me; you *were* a lucky man until tonight."

Azalei spat at Quentin's feet then looked at Gautreau. "Everyone in Vermillion Parish will get an eye full of us having a good old time. Buck naked and buck wild."

"I should never have dirtied my hands getting involved with a— " Gautreau sputtered and choked on his rage.

"Your hands and every other part of your body," Azalei shot back. "Your wife, the judge's daughter, will not be happy. Let me go, and none of this will come out."

"You can get a new wife, Brad," Quentin said.

LaShaun looked at Quentin. His crooked malicious smile sent a chill down her back. Quentin's voice held a whispery quality. The lilting accent was not his own, but one LaShaun found familiar. He eyes gleamed with an unnatural radiance. Quentin's aura turned various shades of red, the colors of anger and a lack of compassion. He walked toward LaShaun with a broad smile. His head tilted oddly to one side.

"Yes, love. I'm here. Your grandmother wanted us to be together," Quentin's mouth spoke the words of another. His voice changed completely. "You must have known I'd come for you."

Brad looked at Quentin and frowned. "What's wrong with you, man?"

"LaShaun, everything can be yours. But you must choose. I can be either one of these men you want. We'll have nothing but days of passion and fun. We can travel the world. I would love for you to see my native land."

"Haiti?" LaShaun gazed at him, mesmerized by the loa.

"I go back much farther, centuries in your time. Zanzibar. I traveled with the slaves to Haiti." Quentin's face twisted. His voice broke through. "What is happening?"

"You're being ridden by an evil spirit called a loa, but you can fight back," LaShaun said loudly. "You have a strong will."

Quentin's expression smoothed out again and his laugh was musical. "Yes, he does, but not stronger than me of course. His streak of evil serves me well."

Gautreau looked at Quentin. "This is a bunch of bull! You're not foolin' me with that phony voodoo act. Quentin, straighten up or I'm gonna shoot you, too."

"That's not Quentin. He's possessed by a being who doesn't care who gets hurt. He might shoot us all," LaShaun said to Gautreau.

"Why are you talking so crazy? Quit playing around, Quentin." When he cackled and made a weird face at her, Azalei shook with terror.

"I had fun with you, girlie. You like to play dirty games with Papa Limba." Quentin winked at her.

"This can't be real. This can't be real." Azalei panted as she looked at him.

Chase faced Gautreau. "Corruption charges are bad, but not as bad as accessory to murder. We both know Quentin mostly likely killed his own grandfather.

Murdering Rita probably came easy for him."

The being in Quentin laughed and turned to LaShaun. "The man of yours still hasn't figured it out. Tsk, tsk, you've chosen quite a dense lover."

Chase shook his head. "Brad, you're willing to kill us to hide an affair? Think, man. Three lives."

LaShaun stared at Gautreau coldly. The scene fell into place inside her head like a movie. "No, that would be four for you, wouldn't it, *Deputy Gautreau*. You killed Rita. I'll bet you were furious when you found out they'd left Azalei alive. You let Azalei think it was all a plan so she wouldn't be suspicious that you got her out there with Rita. She thought she was luring Rita into a trap. But the trap was for both of them."

Quentin clapped his hands and danced around. "Yes, yes. My clever beauty. This Broussard fellow is not worthy of such a queen."

"You dirty sons of bitches," Azalei screamed.

"The forensic guys found swamp grass and mud on Rita's body," Chase said.

"Yeah, so what?" Brad frowned at him.

"GPS," Chase said. "All the units have them because we cover Vermillion Parish, lots of rural areas not close to anything. Using GPS means dispatch can locate us in case an officer is in trouble and can't respond. We can check where your cruiser was at the time of Rita's death."

"Not to mention getting mud from your tires, under your cruiser, maybe even find trace evidence at your house," LaShaun added.

"You have a serious problem, Deputy Gautreau." The loa let out a rumbling laugh that sounded strange coming from deep in Quentin's throat. His voice contained an eerie mix of two distinct timbres. "Most of the evidence points to you and Miss Azalei. This cunning man I own will get away clean." He clapped his hands did a few dance steps again. He spun the gun on one finger like a gunslinger in an old western movie.

"Shut the hell up, Trosclair." Gautreau blinked when large beads of sweat rolled into his eyes.

"No, I'm having too much fun."

Still wearing a spine-chilling grin, Quentin pulled the trigger. Gautreau gave a loud grunt of pain and keeled over against his cruiser. He slid to the ground clutching his neck. Blood sprayed out then poured over his hand. Chase pulled a small gun from an ankle holster. Quentin jerked then staggered as the gun slipped from his fingers. Azalei crawled across the ground like a spider and picked it up gun. She pointed it first at Quentin, then at LaShaun.

"I'll kill her, just try me," Azalei screeched when Chase confronted her. "Everything I got was second hand from you, including him." She jerked her head at Quentin.

"Don't be stupid," LaShaun said, watching the gun instead of her cousin.

"Stupid, huh? I've got the gun," Azalei yelled back.

"You think *I* was stupid enough to come out here without back-up, Azalei?" Chase jerked his head to the right.

"Drop the gun." Deputy Arceneaux emerged from behind a tree. Two more deputies flanked her on the right and left. All three held their weapons in the typical law enforcement stance, with both hands and their legs apart.

"They're trained marksman. This isn't a gunfight you can win, Azalei. Gautreau and Quentin killed Rita. No matter what you feel toward me that must mean something. The Rousselles might cheat each other out of money, but spill each other's blood? No." LaShaun shook her head slowly.

Azalei's entire body shook like she was chilled to the bone. She panted hard, looking first at Gautreau then at Quentin. "What do I do?"

"I'll help you, sweet," Quentin said. He managed to stagger to his feet.

"Azalei, don't." LaShaun tried to close the space between them, but did not make it in time.

"Quentin?" Azalei blinked at him as he approached.

"Of course it's me. I was just throwing them off guard with that act. Now give me the gun." Quentin smiled at her.

Azalei gazed at him steadily. When he was only inches away, the being in Quentin hissed like a snake. Azalei backed up. "No, get away!"

But it was too late. The loa roared from Quentin's mouth. Azalei and he wrestled over the gun. LaShaun shouted the prayer calling on all her force to intervene. Chase leaped forward to grab Quentin. With another roar, the possessed man lifted Chase from the ground effortlessly tossing him away as if he weighed nothing. LaShaun recited the prayer in Creole French that Monmon Odette had left in her diary, a mix of Catholicism, and the old ways from Africa. Distracted Quentin turned to her. The loa answered her in Creole French, the voice like a clap of thunder. Yet, even as LaShaun continued to pray Quentin stumbled

"You cannot turn against me! I am here and will never leave you! No. No," he croaked.

Seeing her chance, Azalei struck him hard on the head. Quentin turned with a growl of rage. He clutched Azalei's arm and bent it back with a snarl. "You will not hurt her."

"I'll kill both of you tonight," Azalei shouted.

She and Quentin struggled over the gun once more. LaShaun raised her voice and the longer she spoke the words, the more Quentin seemed to weaken. Just as he stumbled again Azalei tried to raise the gun. Chase was shouting something to her, but LaShaun only saw his lips moving. A gauze-like veil seemed to drop around her as she continued the prayer. The loa hissed once more, lost his grip on Azalei, and stumbled again. When Chase ran toward them LaShaun watched the scene play out as if in slow motion. She tried to scream at him to stop, but the thick midnight air seemed to suck in the sound. The gunshot broke the spell. Suddenly her vision and hearing sharpened. A scream of pain sent a thrill of fear up her spine. LaShaun ran toward Chase as he stumbled with the unconscious Quentin in his arms.

"Are you hurt?"

"No," he panted. "See if she's okay."

LaShaun raced over to Azalei while Chase let Quentin fall to the ground. He went to Gautreau and knelt beside him. Azalei whimpered when LaShaun touched her. After carefully examining her cousin, LaShaun looked at Chase.

"Far as I can tell the bullet grazed her right side. Lot of blood, but it's just a surface wound," LaShaun said.

Azalei gripped LaShaun's arm. "Don't let me die,

LaShaun. Please."

"You'll be nice and healthy when you go to prison." LaShaun worked free of her cousin's desperate clutch.

Azalei's pretense of fear and pain dissolved into malevolence as she tried to claw LaShaun's face. "I'll make you pay, bi--"

LaShaun spun and cut off her words with a backhand slap across Azalei's face. Her cousin's fear and pain became genuine in an instant as she whimpered and curled into a ball on in the grass.

As though background noise from far away she heard Chase talking the other deputies. Acting Chief Arceneaux gave orders to the dispatcher on Gautreau's radio for the paramedics. LaShaun went to Quentin. Blood stained the dirt and gravel around him. He did not move or give any sign of life as he lay on his side. Then his head turned to her His glassy stare made LaShaun shiver.

"I protected you. How dare she try to hurt you." Then his eyes closed slowly. Seconds later they opened again and he let out a shuddering groan. "LaShaun, please help me."

LaShaun pulled away sharply, disoriented by the change in him. Still she knew the second voice well. The loa had fled the wounded, frail human host and Quentin was free. Chase left Gautreau to check on Quentin. His hands were steady, but his handsome face was pale and shiny with perspiration.

"A couple of paramedic units and more deputies are on the way." Chase looked down at Quentin with no sympathy. "He'll survive."

"What about Gautreau?" LaShaun glanced at the

deputy. He lay in the dirt on his back.

"He's dead," Chase whispered close to her ear. Then he put an arm around her waist. "This has been one hell of a night, but we're okay. We're going to be just fine."

LaShaun trembled and leaned against his solid chest. She stared off into the woods. Wondering if she'd finally banished the evil her family set in motion, and she had unwittingly helped get stronger. She silently prayed that her efforts would keep those around her safe.

* * *

Two days later Beau Chene was still buzzing with the news. CNN, Fox, and even BBC America came to grab every juicy morsel from the residents eager to share gossip. As LaShaun arrived at the Sheriff's office to give one last statement, a pretty female reporter hurried over to her.

"Ms. Rousselle, I'm Keitha Peters with Fox News Louisiana." The young woman spoke quickly while motioning a videographer into position.

"Nice to meet you. No comment." LaShaun brushed past her while the reporter called out questions.

Chase met her halfway on the stone steps leading into the station. He blocked the camera view of LaShaun with his body. ". Come this way."

"Deputy Broussard, is it true you killed a demon to protect the woman you love?" The reporter yelled before the pushed through the glass doors into the station.

"Great. My career has been reduced to a tabloid

headline," Chase grumbled.

"Sorry you got mixed up like this," LaShaun said and glanced up at him briefly,

"Mostly I was doing my job," he replied in his best official tone. But he gave her hand a squeeze before letting it go when they reached his boss's office.

Chase knocked once then opened the door. The wide office had two windows that let in plenty of sunshine. Pictures of smiling children framed in silver were scattered atop three big file cabinets. Strange to find such a cheerful room in a place where dark deeds were discussed. To her surprise, Sheriff Triche sat behind his desk. Mable Arceneaux stood at attention to his right, her arms crossed behind her.

"Well, well. Ain't the last two days been a real mess." Sheriff Triche grimaced at LaShaun.

"Yes, sir." LaShaun looked at Chase then back to the older man .

"I knew Brad Gautreau all his life. Always had a wild streak, but I never would have figured." The sheriff heaved a sigh. He picked up his ringing phone then slammed it back down without speaking. "Damn reporters."

Deputy Arceneaux cleared her throat. "Trosclair blames Gautreau for everything, especially the murder. He and Azalei are lawyered up."

"What about Azalei?" LaShaun asked.

"She'll be charged with accessory before and after a crime and a few other things. Too bad being a scheming witch isn't against the law. She'd get twenty to life on that one," Deputy Arceneaux said dryly.

"Trosclair kept his hands pretty clean. We're working on what we have on him. Those knot-heads

Azalei hired to go after you will likely give us something." Sheriff Triche grunted. "I'll get him if it's the last thing I do before I retire."

"I warned him you're like a pit bull, once you clamp down on something with those jaws you won't let go. So, what does the DA say about me?" LaShaun looked at Deputy Arceneaux and back at Sheriff Triche.

"Go home," he said gruffly. "And try not to cause any more trouble, a least for the next few days. Stretch it out to a few months if you can. As for you Broussard, you may have missed your chance to be elected. But that's the least of your worries. I may think up several good reasons to reprimand you for insubordination and not being forthcoming with Mable. She was your superior officer, or did that slip your mind?"

"No, sir." Chase pressed his lips together.

"Chase didn't do anything wrong." LaShaun looked at him. "He— "

"We'll decide on that, young lady." Sheriff Triche cut her off. "And don't either of you go blabbing to them damn reporters. Stories about sex and voodoo on the bayou. I'd like to wring their necks. Go on now, outta my sight." He waved at them to leave.

Deputy Arceneaux shrugged then shook her head when Chase started to speak. He looked at his boss. The Sheriff's angry bulldog expression seemed to convince him. Chase opened the door and followed LaShaun out.

"So that's it then. The fiasco is over." Chase let out a long slow breath.

"That's a joke, right?" LaShaun said as she faced him.

"Yeah, and the town will be talking about this for weeks," he agreed.

"For years." LaShaun continued to gaze at him. "What you did for me, I appreciate it but— "

"Like my boss said, I can take care of myself." Chase replied, his deep voice firm. "About what happened with Quentin, I mean. That... thing that took control of him. Was that real?

LaShaun nodded. "Very."

"Is it gone for good?"

She looked past him into another realm, the one her grandmother had reached into with dangerous results. She knew that once disturbed, those forces were not so easily stopped. Then she placed a hand on his chest. She pushed his collar aside to see the leather cord around his neck. LaShaun was relieved to feel the outline of the pendant she'd given him.

"I hope it won't come back," LaShaun said quietly.

"I think the worst is over," he said.

His husky scent and deep voice brought her back to this world. Looking into his Cajun dark eyes helped bring the sunshine back into her life. Good had been stronger. No matter how many times midnight arrived a new day full of promise would return. They ignored the stares of the other deputies and the civilian employees.

"The Sheriff ordered us to leave. With all these reporters around we can't go anywhere too public." LaShaun raised an eyebrow at him.

"Maybe they haven't found my place," Chase said.

"Of course they have. Somebody is bound to have told them where you live."

He grinned. "But I'll bet they don't know about the camp on False River my great-aunt left me in her will. It's fixed up with all the comforts of home."

Two hours later, they lay wrapped around each other in the bed of the master bedroom. The "camp" was more like a lovely old house with three bedrooms, a kitchen, and a porch facing the water. The occasional hum of boat motors going by sounded soothing. Chase kissed her neck and tried to snuggle even closer.

"I've ruined your chance to be elected sheriff." LaShaun looked up at him.

"I wouldn't say that. Haven't you heard? I'm a hero in Beau Chene. I caught a killer and faced down a demon." Chase laughed when she rolled her eyes.

"Oh I can't believe you just said that." LaShaun pressed her lips to the pendant on the cord around his neck.

"I'm just repeating the headlines. Even the mayor is giving interviews, so don't assume I'll have to leave town." Chase put a finger under her chin and lifted her face. "You can't get rid of me now."

"Well, since I'm stuck with you," LaShaun whispered. She put both arms around his naked waist. "I might as well make the best of it."

Read more LaShaun Rousselle Mysteries

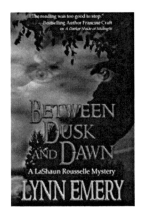

About the Author

    Mix knowledge of voodoo, Louisiana politics and forensic social work with the dedication to write fiction while working each day as a clinical social worker, and you get a snapshot of author Lynn Emery. Lynn has been a contributing consultant to the magazine *Today's Black Woman* for three articles about contemporary relationships between black men and women. For more information visit:

www.lynnemery.com

CPSIA information can be obtained at www.ICGtesting.com
Printed in the USA
LVOW13s2343210114

370320LV00001B/3/P